The Plan

by
Samantha Powers

The Capitol Love Series
Book 1

ISBN: 978-0986182242

Published and distributed
by Possibilities Publishing Company

www.possibilitiespublishingcompany.com

This is a work of fiction.

For Kevin. This story wouldn't exist without you. Your influence lives throughout these pages, and you live on in my heart forever.

For Chris. You are my everything. Forever.

Chapter 1

"This is the beginning," Savannah whispered. "This is when everything starts."

She wrapped her arms around herself and squeezed to suppress the urge to shout "WaHOO!" and twirl like a character in a Disney movie. Since it was not quite 6 a.m. on a Saturday, she figured her new roommates would be less than amused if she woke them by whooping and jumping around on the porch.

But it took real effort to resist because today was *it*. Her *real* life was finally starting. Today.

Dressed in her pink cotton pajama shorts and tank top, Savannah propped her bare feet on the bottom rung of the porch railing and leaned out to see if she could get a glimpse of the U.S. Capitol building a few blocks away, just on the other side of those trees and buildings. Despite having lived in the D.C. area for her entire life—first growing up in Fairfax, Virginia, and then going to school at George Washington University—everything still felt completely new. She was living in the heart of the city, on Capitol Hill, and on her own! No parents, no dorm, no classes. The urge to shout and twirl welled up in her again.

Unable to stay still any longer, Savannah flung her arms out and started to dance around on the front porch of her new home. Hesitantly at first but then enjoying the sensation of the balmy early-summer air on her skin, she threw her head back and twirled around faster and faster until she lost her balance and collapsed giggling against the side railing of the porch.

At the sound of clapping, she jerked her head up to see that she had an audience. A guy—correction, a super-hot guy—was standing on the sidewalk. He wore a black T-shirt and faded jeans and had a Nationals baseball cap pulled low over his brow. And he was smiling the most dazzling smile.

"I give it a 7.5," he said.

Mortified that a total stranger had just watched her prancing around in her PJs, Savannah started to sidle to the door. But then she reminded herself that this was the beginning of her new life. So instead she rose up to her full height of 5-foot-4 and said, "Wow, harsh!"

Mr. Sexy chuckled and said, "Anyone can twirl. I'm looking for personality."

"Oh really?" Savannah swept her long chestnut hair into a messy bun. "What if I did this?"

She stood on her left leg with her left arm stretched out in front of her and reached back to grab her right ankle with her other hand. She wobbled a moment but then steadied herself and tipped forward in the classic dancer's pose from yoga, stretching her leg back as far as she could and thrusting her chest forward.

She held her breath and glanced toward the sidewalk to see if he was watching. He was, and he was still smiling, which gave her a little thrill. But that slight movement of her head was enough to upset her balance and she started to tip over. She reached for the wicker chair beside her, but it skittered away when she tried to grab it, and she tumbled to the floor.

Before she could collect herself, Savannah heard the front door open and cringed.

"NO. Just...no."

Savannah looked up to see Carol, one of her new roommates and the owner of the house, standing in the doorway with a threadbare bathrobe belted around her waist. Her eyes were puffy with sleep, her short red hair was tousled, and she was looking utterly unimpressed with Savannah's performance.

"This?" Carol waved a finger as if drawing an imaginary line around Savannah. "With the noise and the energy and the 6 a.m.? Not OK."

Carol went back inside, letting the door close behind her with a bang. Savannah stood and turned back to Sir Hotness on the sidewalk, who held her gaze for a long second before they both burst out laughing.

Then with a slight bow and a tip of his baseball cap, he continued on his way, and Savannah, still chuckling and feeling even more in love with the potential of her new life, hurried inside. She nearly crashed into Carol, who was carrying a mug of steaming hot coffee and who repeated "No" before disappearing down the stairs to her basement room. Savannah's best friend—and other roommate—Rayne had warned her that Carol could be grumpy, so Savannah didn't pay much attention, and instead smiled and skipped up the stairs to her room to get dressed. She wanted to be ready when her parents arrived to help her move the rest of her stuff into her new home.

Chapter 2

Colin could never be accused of being a morning person, but if he had to be up and working at the crack of dawn, this was the kind of morning to do it on. Late May in the District meant you could feel summer lurking just around the corner, but the early mornings still had the cool crispness of spring. In fact, that was often the only place spring weather existed because winter seemed to move almost immediately into swampy summer if you were a late riser.

The satisfaction of knowing he'd already worked harder than most people would all day made the morning even sweeter. The addition of the super-cute twirling girl was an unexpected bonus.

Whistling, he picked up his pace as he headed to Sweet Happens Café to grab a quick breakfast before starting the second part of his workday.

As he walked inside, Crystal, the café's owner, greeted him with a warm smile. "Colin! Perfect timing. I just took the croissants out of the oven."

"That is not accidental," he said with a smile.

Crystal was nearly as tall as him, with short, spiky black hair and big dark eyes. She moved with the grace and athleticism of a dancer, and he'd always admired that about her.

"Help yourself to coffee," she said, handing him a to-go cup.

Colin turned toward the self-serve machines across from the counter, and Crystal said, "I'm also going to give you a blueberry banana scone. It's a new recipe, and I want to know what you think."

"Well, if you insist," Colin said as the bakery began to fill with the scent of hazelnut coffee.

"Hey, ah." Even though they were clearly the only people in

the tiny bakery, Colin still paused to look around and dropped his voice slightly before continuing. "Everything go OK with that delivery yesterday?"

Crystal matched his quiet tone. "Yes, thank you. You really did me a solid. I don't know how I would have made it through the day otherwise."

"Happy to help," Colin said with a smile.

The door opened and a gray-haired man in a gray suit walked in, followed by a woman in yoga pants pushing a sleepy toddler in a stroller. Colin stirred some sugar and cream into his coffee and popped on a plastic lid.

Crystal came over and handed him a white paper bag. "I threw an extra croissant in there for your brother," she said.

"Chase? He's still in whatever godforsaken country he ran off to a few weeks ago."

Crystal smiled. "I'm pretty sure I saw him walk by when I was opening up this morning."

"Well, shows what I know." He hesitated then said, "You know you can do much better than Chase, right?" He hoped his voice sounded light even though he was very serious. Crystal had been carrying a torch for his charming but flaky brother since a brief fling a few months ago.

"Like who? You?" Crystal teased.

"Ah, you know I never mix business and pleasure." Colin winked at her and then headed out the door.

Chapter 3

"Dad! Let me carry that—you'll hurt yourself!" Savannah called as she tried to run ahead of her father, who was carrying a box with a suitcase perched on top and feeling his way for the first step up to her porch.

"I've got it, sweets. Just because you're suddenly all grown up doesn't mean I'm suddenly too old to do anything." He let out a hearty chuckle as he successfully navigated the first step and moved to the second.

"Daddy, this isn't about you being old—it's about the fact that you can't see," she protested.

"I've got eyes in my feet!"

She was about to argue again when her mother came out onto the porch and said, "Oh, Savannah, relax. If he gets hurt, it's his funeral. Isn't that right, John?"

"As always, Marianne," he said with a smile. He reached the porch and paused to lean out from behind his load to give Savannah's mom a quick kiss before going through the doorway into the house.

"Yeah, but it's my stuff that's going to get dropped!" Savannah muttered as she turned back to the truck and pulled out another suitcase. Her mother walked down from the porch to join her.

"Darling, I moved your bed away from the window," she said, sliding a small box out of the truck. "It was too drafty for you there."

"Mom, I just put the bed there. I spent most of the night arranging the room," Savannah said. "I think it will be nice to wake up to the sunlight."

"You'll get a head cold after two days. Is that how you want to start your fancy new job?"

"It's SUMMER!" Savannah called after her mother, who was already climbing up the porch steps.

"Technically, I think it's still considered spring," said a deep and vaguely familiar voice behind her.

Savannah spun around, and her stomach dropped when she realized it was Mr. McSexy from that morning. After an awkward, speechless moment, she brushed a loose strand of hair from her face and said, "Whose side are you on anyway?"

"Not taking sides, just stating a fact," he said with a smile, shoving his hands into his pockets.

He'd changed into a charcoal gray T-shirt and ditched his baseball cap, and Savannah was trying not to stare at his intensely blue eyes and the way the late morning sun bounced off his short but slightly shaggy brown hair. The T-shirt also revealed the edge of a tattoo on his right biceps and another on the inside of his left forearm that she hadn't noticed that morning.

"Hello there! Are you one of Nanna's city friends?" Savannah's dad had suddenly appeared behind her. Her face flushed red at his use of her childhood nickname, on top of his assumption that this beautiful man was a friend of hers.

"We could use a little more muscle. Nanna's better at supervising than carrying things," her dad said with a good-natured laugh and a squeeze of Savannah's shoulder.

"No, Dad! He's not...uh, he's just passing by. He's not helping." Savannah knew she was bright red down to her toes and prayed that Mr. Hotty would just quietly disappear.

"I'm in no rush," he said. "I'd be happy to help, sir."

"I'm not going to say no to a few less trips up those stairs," her dad said as he moved toward the truck.

"NO!" Savannah said a little more shrilly than she had intended. "I don't want you to be late for... that thing…"

In her desperation, she grabbed his arm to turn him toward the street. "You know...that thing you were telling me…" Her voice trailed off as she felt him flex his biceps under her hand, and she had an overwhelming urge to push up his sleeve so she could see the rest of his tattoo. Instead, she dropped her hand and took a step back. His smile faltered, and he looked surprised, confused even.

"Right. Yes, that *thing*," he said, then leaned past her to catch her father's eye and said, "Sorry, sir. I hope you'll be able to manage on your own."

"Oh sure, I've got mad skills. Isn't that how you say it?" her dad asked.

"It sure is, sir. And I'm sure you do. I guess I'll catch you later...Nanna," Mr. Sexy said with a wink.

Savannah smiled but didn't meet his gaze and quickly turned to help her father.

Several physically and mentally exhausting hours later, she waved as her parents pulled away from the curb and headed back home to Fairfax. Too tired to move another inch, she sank down on the steps and rested her head against the railing, wondering what Carol would do if she found her asleep right there.

"Hey! Did I miss Marianne and John?!" Rayne asked as she ran up the sidewalk from the direction of the Metro.

"By about 20 seconds. And don't think for one second that I believe it was an accident," Savannah said, shooting Rayne a pretend annoyed face. Her friend was very familiar with the chaos that swirled around John and Marianne from their years of being roommates at George Washington.

"I swear I did not get called into work today on purpose. I really wanted to help! But hopefully this will make up for it." Rayne handed Savannah a white bakery box.

"Sweet Happens?" Savannah said, reading the teal-and-brown label on the box.

"It's an amazing bakery down by the corner. I never noticed it before, but my boss was raving about the cupcakes the other day and then just now I realized that I walk past it every day."

Savannah laughed as she ripped through the tape on the box lid. Rayne often existed inside her head more than outside it and was always failing to notice things that were right in front of her.

"Sheesh, right," Savannah said around the caramel mocha cupcake she had shoved into her mouth.

"Good! So the sugar rush should give you the energy to go get showered and get dinner with me?"

Nodding, mouth full, Savannah stood and started up the stairs, then turned back to Rayne. She motioned to the box, indicating that she was keeping the other three cupcakes, too.

"Of course," Rayne said with a smile as she followed Savannah upstairs.

Chapter 4

"So what awesome Capitol Hill restaurant are you introducing me to tonight?" Savannah asked an hour later as she lay on her stomach on Rayne's bed, freshly showered and wearing the first clean clothes she could lay her hands on—white capri jeans and a loose-fitting pink tank top.

"I was thinking of the burger place down on 4th," Rayne said as she slipped on dangly shell earrings. She was wearing a hand-embroidered smock top with faded jeans and sandals.

"Is it a chain?"

Rayne hesitated. "It's a local one—"

"NO!"

"You won't even know it's a chain! It's really trendy!" Rayne argued, despite knowing it was pointless. She and Savannah had been having the chain versus non-chain argument for four years, practically since the moment they'd met in college. Rayne was two years ahead of Savannah, but they'd quickly become friends and stayed close even after Rayne had graduated and moved to this house on Capitol Hill.

"Rayne, what do we say about chains?"

"That they are predictable, affordable, and comforting?" Rayne asked as she ran a brush through her chin-lenth hair, which framed her face with waves in a rich chocolate brown.

"Come on, say it with me: 'Chain restaurants are what the suburbs are for.'"

But instead of saying it with Savannah, Rayne rolled her eyes then picked up her purse from the dresser. They'd done this routine multiple times over the years.

Laughing, Savannah got up from the bed, grabbed Rayne in a vigorous hug, and said, "Aren't you SO glad we're living together again, Rayne?!"

Unable to maintain her pretend annoyance, Rayne hugged Savannah back and said, "I really am."

"OK, well, I'm wearing your sparkly flip-flops because I can't find any of my shoes, and then you are taking me someplace Capitol Hill-ish."

"A food truck it is then!" Rayne said as they made their way down the stairs and out the front door.

When they reached the sidewalk, Rayne steered Savannah toward Eastern Market. "I've got an idea," she said. "Why don't you use your spidey sense to find us our new favorite restaurant?"

"Yes! I'll find us our new Mulligans," Savannah said, referring to the bar that had been their second home when they were in college and had led to the discovery of Savannah's "superpower": finding the perfect bar or restaurant no matter what city they were in.

A few blocks later, Savannah came to a stop. "Here."

"Here?" Rayne followed Savannah's gaze to a slightly run-down townhouse with bay windows jutting out on either side of the stairs. The wrought-iron railings were rusted and shedding black paint in places. The word "Zipped" was scrawled across the beat-up front door, looking more like an act of vandalism than an act of marketing.

"I can feel it," Savannah said. She ran up the stairs knowing that Rayne would eventually follow.

Once inside, a slow smile spread across Savannah's face. In contrast to the shabby exterior, the interior was warm, polished, and classy without being stuffy.

"Definitely here," she said as Rayne came up beside her.

Savannah surveyed the room, trying to decide if she wanted to sit at a round table in a bay window, one of the small square tables with mismatched chairs scattered around the center of the room, or one of the groups of wingback chairs toward the back. She decided on the bar, where she could talk to the bartender and get a better feel for the place.

As Savannah and Rayne settled themselves on two high-backed stools at the center of the U-shaped bar, a waitress in a black T-shirt, black jeans, spiky pink hair, and earrings covering all of both ears came through the doorway to the left of the bar.

"Hey, guys! The bartender will be right out," she said cheerfully, carrying a tray piled with mac and cheese and cornbread to the only other patrons in the place—two men in suits who looked to be in their thirties.

"Oh, that. I need that," Savannah said, turning on her stool to watch as the tray moved across the room and came to rest on the men's table. While she was debating how weird it would be if she went over and asked for a taste, she heard a voice that was becoming very familiar say, "Hello, ladies. What can I get for you?"

Savannah turned back to the bar to see her gorgeous stranger.

"Hey!" she said and immediately blushed at her eloquence.

"Hey yourself!" he said with a smile as he set down cocktail napkins, seemingly unfazed at running into her yet again.

"Do you guys know each other?" Rayne asked.

"No!" Savannah said just as he said, "Yeah."

"I mean, yes...I guess. Sort of..." Savannah felt her face growing hot again. So much for the "new" Savannah. She was just as bumbling and nervous around this man as she'd been around every attractive boy who had ever talked to her in high school or college.

Rayne looked from the bartender to Savannah, waiting for one of them to fill her in. But he just smiled at Savannah for a moment before setting two menus on the bar.

"Why don't I give you two a second to look over the menu?" he said and moved to the far end of the bar.

Rayne looked at Savannah. "You're going to explain that, but first, can I just say how not surprised I am that you have been here less than 24 hours and you already have a story that involves one of the hottest men I've ever seen in real life?"

"Oh my god, right? So I'm not imagining it! It's like he walked right out of a magazine."

"Definitely not imagining it," Rayne said as she eyed the view of his backside that he was providing from his post at the far end of the bar. "So?"

Lowering her voice, Savannah told Rayne about her two encounters with him that day.

"And you didn't get his name?" Rayne asked.

"No. I've taken to calling him Mr. Sexy in my head."

"Clever."

From the other end of the bar, they heard, "Mr. Sexy is so formal. Why don't you just call me Colin?"

Savannah felt her body temperature skyrocket and the heat move from her face down her chest and arms. Despite applying all her mental powers to making Colin stay where he was, he sauntered back to them. Leaning his forearms on the bar and focusing his magnetic blue eyes on her, he said, "Don't you think? Nanna?"

"Oh god!" Savannah said and dropped her forehead to the bar so that she was staring at the floor. "This can't possibly get any more embarrassing."

"Ohhhhh, I'm the only non-family member allowed to call her that!" Rayne said. "See, her head is down like that because she's searching her purse for her switch blade. She'll cut you."

"Well, since she hasn't told me her real name, I have to work with what I've got."

Savannah waited for Rayne to tell him her name. Or say something to make him go away. Anything. But as the silence stretched, her curiosity got the better of her, and she slowly lifted her head to find herself staring into those hypnotizing blue eyes.

After a beat, Colin's mouth twitched up into a crooked smile. "No? Still not going to tell me your name? Well, that's cool. I'll wait. In the meantime, I'll get started on your drinks."

As soon as his eyes let go of hers, Savannah's voice—and brain—returned. "But we didn't order anything!"

"No worries, Red," he said, turning to look at her down the length of the bar. "I can tell what people need to be drinking. It's one of my superpowers."

Savannah tried to ignore the heat that was spreading from her belly and out through her veins. "Red? My hair is brown."

"I wasn't talking about your hair," he said.

Rayne burst out laughing, and Savannah narrowed her eyes at her. "I will definitely cut *you*."

Later that evening, as Rayne and Savannah walked home in the cool night air, stomachs full of comfort food and heads slightly buzzed from comfort drinks, Rayne said, "So. Colin," with a smile and a nudge.

"So? Colin?" Savannah said, trying to sound nonchalant.

"Heeee liiikes youuuu!" Rayne sang and threw her arm around Savannah.

"Whatever. He does not. He's just...one of those guys. A player. A charmer. It's a survival skill for a bartender." Savannah tried to ignore the butterflies that took flight in her stomach at the thought of him.

"Hmmmmm, maybe. Maybe not." Rayne giggled and hip-butted Savannah, who then had to steady Rayne back on her feet.

"It doesn't matter. I mean, yeah, he's super hot—"

"Insanely hot!"

"But, I mean, he has tattoos—"

"Sexy tattoos."

"And he's a bartender—"

"A sexy bartender."

"Rayne! This isn't a call-and-response rap. I'm saying he's not my type. He doesn't fit The Plan."

"Oh right! THE PLAN!" Rayne said in a deep voice while raising a fist in the air.

Savannah put her arm around Rayne to help her up the steps of their porch and onto the swing by the front door.

"The plan is good," Savannah said as Rayne leaned her head on her shoulder. "And it's already in motion." She raised her hand and started ticking items off on her fingers. "I've got the place in the city. I start my job as a program manager at the Capitol Foundation next week, which gives me plenty of time and opportunity to advance and build my path toward being an executive director of a major foundation by the time I'm forty. All I need is the guy—professional, driven, responsible. Maybe a lawyer or a policy analyst, and we'll renovate a row house by Eastern Market and—"

The sound of snoring coming from Rayne interrupted Savannah's fantasy.

"Shut up!" she said as she shoved her friend.

"Oh, did I nod off during your fascinating recitation of The Plan? Did you get to the part about the wainscoting in the breakfast nook yet? Because I love that part."

Savannah pinched Rayne's arm playfully, but Rayne pulled away and stood up.

"Look, all I'm saying is The Plan is...the plan. I'm sure you'll follow it and live happily ever after, but isn't there room for a little fun with the sexy bartender before your appointment with the realtor?"

Every part of Savannah screamed Yes! but she crossed her arms and narrowed her eyes at Rayne. "No. The Plan exists for a reason. We both know what that reason is."

Rayne did know. That had been a hard year for both of them. With a sigh, she bent down and wrapped her arms around Savannah in a clumsy hug. "Welcome home, babe!" she said. Then she turned toward the door. "Does the plan allow for going to bed at 8:30 on a Saturday night when you worked all day? Because, you know, if it's going to threaten The Plan, I can totally—"

"Go to bed, Rayne!" Savannah said, laughing and adding an affectionate "dork" just before the door closed.

She pulled her knees up to her chest, wrapped her arms around her legs, watched as night settled over her new neighborhood and tried not to think about those magnetic blue eyes or those tattoos that she really wanted to see the rest of— and find out if any more were lurking in less visible places. The thought of Colin's less visible places sent a slight shiver through her body. Instead of letting her mind wander down that path any further, she decided to go inside and eat the rest of the cupcakes Rayne had brought her.

Colin wiped down the bar for the third time and readied the

already organized back bar for the next morning—and finally admitted to himself that he was stalling until he could come up with an excuse to walk past Red's house on his way home, even though it was three blocks in the wrong direction. He knew she felt the same spark he did when they were near each other. He'd felt it as soon as she'd turned those amazing green eyes on him that morning. But she kept pulling back. He'd never had to work very hard to get the attention—or affection—of women. But he could already sense that she was different. And it made him want to get to know her even more.

Chapter 5

After closing the bar the night before, 4 a.m. came much too quickly for Colin, but he had work to do. Two hours later, tired and in need of a shower, he turned the corner onto Savannah's street. He told himself it was highly unlikely she'd be awake or out on the porch again. He told himself he was only walking past her house because it was the fastest route home if he wanted to stop at Sweet Happens, not because he was acting like a lovesick teenager trying to get a look at his crush. Except that when he turned the corner and saw her, his heart sped up and his mouth went a little dry.

She'd traded those cute pajamas for gray sweat pants and a pink tank top, and she was struggling down the porch steps backward tugging a large, awkward-looking box full of flattened boxes and packing paper.

Colin quickly closed the few hundred yards between them and came up the steps behind her.

"Hi!" he said.

Savannah let go of the box with a yelp and spun around with her arms raised in a defensive posture. As soon as she recognized him, she started to relax—and the box started to slide down the stairs behind her. It smacked into the back of her knees, and she pitched forward into Colin, who instinctively wrapped his arms around her, but the momentum pushed him off his feet.

The next thing he knew he was flat on his back with Savannah pressed solidly on top of him.

"Omph!" she said as they landed.

"Did you just say 'omph'?" Colin asked. It felt nice—way too nice—having her on top of him. He wanted to keep her there as long as possible.

"It's what you say when you fall."

"No, it's not," he said with a laugh. "It's a sound one *could* make on impact, but it's not something you actually say."

She propped her forearms on his chest and looked down at him, her chestnut hair falling like a curtain around them. "What are you even doing here? Again. Stalker."

"I'm not a stalker. I was on my way home—this is my way home."

"Just now getting home, huh? I see," she said in a teasing tone.

"What? NO! No, I—"

"Hey, you don't have to explain yourself to me." She started to get up, but his arms were around her and he tightened his grip. When she raised a questioning eyebrow, he chose to continue as if this were a totally natural position for a chat between two virtual strangers.

"I guess I shouldn't complain," she said. "You probably saved my ass."

"Well, it's far too nice an ass to let anything happen to it," he said with a cocky smile, deciding that he didn't care if his attraction to her started to manifest in a noticeable way.

Savannah blushed, and knowing the heat was going to spread through her body, she suddenly felt a strong need to put some space between her and Colin. Feeling something very obvious beginning to press against her belly only increased her urgency. Shifting so that her right knee was on the ground, she placed her hands on either side of his head and started to lever herself off him.

"Whoa, Red. Where do you think you're going?"

With lightning speed, he rolled her onto her back and was now hovering above her—hands on either side of her head, knees braced on the outside of her legs but no part of his body touching hers to give himself a much-needed break. The way Savannah affected him, he was starting to worry that he might complete his transformation into lovesick teenager in a most embarrassing way.

"Wow. That was clearly a practiced move," she said.

"Actually, that's the first time I've ever done that." Colin lowered his head toward hers before adding, "At least while dressed."

"You're very talented," she said, but it took a lot of effort to form coherent thoughts when her brain kept picturing him lowering himself down, slowly, until their—

"Whatcha thinking 'bout there, Red?" Colin whispered, his body now lightly brushing against hers.

Flushing a deeper red at being called out, she couldn't think of anything to say and instead raised her hands to his chest in a vague attempt to create some space between them. But feeling the hard muscles of his chest flex under her fingers only made things worse.

"Are you thinking about all my talents?" he breathed, his mouth barely an inch from hers.

As she calculated how much she'd have to shift until his lips touched hers, she suddenly realized that she was seriously considering kissing a virtual stranger. She was shocked at herself. And a little impressed. But mostly shocked. This was exactly the kind of behavior that would destroy The Plan.

She moved her gaze from his full, enticing lips to his eyes— now more of an indigo blue—but that didn't help. Closing her eyes tight, she cleared her throat and said, "I was thinking about how my garbage is spilled all over the sidewalk and I should really get it picked up."

"Liar." But he knew the mood had shifted. He'd seen a door close behind her eyes.

"You know, holding me here like this could be considered a felony in most states."

"Misdemeanor at best."

"Are you ever going to let me get up?"

"All you had to do was ask, Red." Colin got to his feet in one fluid motion and held a hand out to help her up.

Ignoring the stab of disappointment at his eagerness to let her go, Savannah got up without his help. But it was clear to her now that if she wasn't careful, he would destroy The Plan faster than she could say, "Take me now." And there was no way she was going to let that happen. Moving past him without making eye contact, she began picking up the things that had fallen out of the box and were strewn across the sidewalk and lawn.

Colin started to help her.

"I've got this," she said. "I'm sure you want to get home after your long night out." She heard the edge in her voice and told herself it wouldn't hurt for Colin to think she was bipolar.

"OK, sure. Whatever you want." Colin dropped the flattened cardboard box he'd picked up and headed for the street, irritation replacing arousal. He didn't need this kind of drama. He was just looking for some fun, not a girl who played games.

"See you around, Red," he said when he was a few feet away.

"Do you even know my name?" Savannah called after him.

Colin stopped walking and shoved his hands in his pockets. "You mean it's not Red?"

Savannah rolled her eyes and said, "It's Savannah."

"Great to meet you, Savannah. Enjoy the rest of your day."

Then he darted diagonally across the intersection, aiming for Sweet Happens and hoping some sugar and caffeine would clear his head.

Savannah watched as Colin jogged away, noticing how the muscles in his shoulders and upper arms moved under his closely fitted T-shirt. He wasn't built like someone who spent a lot of time at the gym lifting weights, but his body was surprisingly tight and compact—like a soccer player or a swimmer maybe? Savannah flashed back to lying on top of him and remembered how solid his abs felt against her belly. Her body temperature started to climb again, and she turned her attention to getting her garbage to the curb so she could go back to unpacking her room.

As Colin hustled toward Sweet Happens, he kept replaying the last few minutes in his head, trying to figure out what had happened. One minute she was so clearly on the same overwhelming chemistry page as him, and then bam, she totally shut down. He told himself again that he didn't need to get involved with a crazy chick.

"Screw that," he said out loud.

"Talking to yourself now?"

Colin jumped. Then he turned and saw his brother grinning at him.

"Dude. You scared the crap out of me!" he said as he shook Chase's hand and pulled him in for a man hug.

"I was sure you saw me. I've been standing right here watching you since before you turned the corner. But I guess you were too busy daydreaming like a schoolgirl," Chase teased as he put Colin's head in a playful chokehold.

"Get off me," Colin said, but he was laughing as he ducked away from his brother. "I heard you were back in town. Where've you been hiding out?"

"Eh, you know, here and there," Chase said with a wink.

Chase was the one member of their family who was not pursuing a career in the hospitality industry. Instead, much to their father's and grandfather's consternation, he had become a freelance photojournalist, specializing in extreme landscapes and exotic animals. Which meant he traveled frequently, and that suited him just fine. For the brief periods when he was in town, he shared an apartment with Colin.

"But I must have missed you this morning," Chase said with a waggle of his eyebrows that Colin chose to ignore. He continued on his walk to the bakery, and Chase fell into step beside him.

"That was some serious daydream," Chase said with a grin. "Only two things make you go inside your head like that." He held up two fingers and ticked them off: "work and women." Watching Colin for a reaction, he said, "So how's work?"

Smiling and continuing on his walk to the bakery, Colin said, "Work is fine."

"OK, so what's her damage? A clinger? A cuddler? An over-talker?" When Colin didn't answer, Chase said, "Well, it couldn't have been too bad since you're just now getting home," and slapped him on the back.

"Hey, I've been up since 4. I've been to the waterfront fish market and to work, after working until 2 a.m. last night. Not that you'd know about hard work, Mr. Fancy Photographer Man," Colin teased.

"Yeah, yeah. So fine, then what's this chick done to get you twisted up?"

"Eh. It's nothing. It's not even worth talking about. Just some mixed signals."

"I hear you. Bitches be crazy, right?" Chase said with a laugh.

Colin loved his brother, but he was the very definition of a player. He knew it came from a kind of attention-deficit disorder rather than malevolence or lack of respect. But he wasn't sure the distinction mattered much to the string of broken-hearted women Chase left in his wake.

They reached the patio at Sweet Happens, and Colin noticed his brother had stopped walking. "You coming in?" he asked.

"Yeah, it's probably not a great idea. Right?"

Colin looked through the window and saw Crystal bustling around inside. "Yeah. Probably not. It's pretty busy. I'll tell her you said thanks for the pastry yesterday."

"Cool. I'll catch you later, bro." Chase punched Colin on the shoulder and broke into a jog to cross the street before the light changed.

Shaking his head at his brother, Colin pushed open the door and hoped that Crystal hadn't seen Chase and that if she had, she wouldn't ask why he hadn't come in.

Chapter 6

For the next few days, Savannah kept herself busy settling into her room and the house and getting ready to start her new job the following week. She had unpacked and arranged all her stuff, gone shopping for the final pieces of her new professional wardrobe, and just finished testing her route and commuting time. And most important, she hadn't had any more run-ins with Colin.

She was in the process of congratulating herself on how little thought she'd given to him over the past few days—which is to say not exactly 24/7—when her cell phone rang. Smiling at the sight of Rayne's name on her screen, she answered with a cheerful "Hey!"

"Hey yourself, stranger! Is it weird that we sleep 20 feet from each other but haven't crossed paths in almost three days?"

"I've been busy getting settled," Savannah protested. "I don't want anything to distract me from work when I start on Monday."

"You're such a nerd."

"True. But I've also been sitting at home the last two nights while you've been off doing whatever...or whoever?" Rayne hadn't dated in over a year—not since that mess with a colleague—and Savannah was hoping to hear that things had finally changed.

"Working. Only working. Climate change isn't going to stop itself, you know. But I'm free tonight, so let's hang out."

"Done. Where are you? I'm starving. We need to eat."

"I discovered this little diner you're going to love. Meet me at Independence and 6th in ten?"

"Done!"

Fifteen minutes later, they were sliding into a red pleather booth in a diner that looked like it had been transplanted from the fifties, complete with a fully decked-out soda fountain at the long counter that ran down the middle.

"I'm in love with this place," Savannah declared as she picked up a plastic laminated menu.

"The best part is that they locally source their food and are all about a small footprint and organic food," Rayne said. "It's the charm of the fifties without the environmental destruction."

"Love. It."

After ordering grilled cheese sandwiches, fries, and malteds, Rayne said, "So anything left on your itemized and color-coded to-do list that I can help with?"

"Well, since you asked," Savannah said, taking a deep breath. "Tonight's agenda is to get started meeting boys. Or I guess I should say men."

"Haven't you already started that with Mr. Sexy Bartender?"

"No! I need to start meeting men based on my checklist. I know I'm not going to find him right away, so I need to start looking now. It could seriously take years."

The waiter arrived with their food. Savannah took a bite of the gooey sandwich and thought she'd found heaven.

"I still don't see why you can't have a little fun before starting that particular part of The Plan," Rayne said between bites.

"Nothing says these appropriate men won't also be fun."

"I'm pretty sure everything says that."

Savannah pointed a french fry at her. "Do you want to hear my plan or not?"

"Definitely," Rayne said, taking a long sip of her malted. "I can't wait to hear The Plan to find the man for The Plan."

"I'm ignoring your mocking. Tonight I'm setting up online dating profiles and looking for some meet-ups for single young professionals." Savannah paused to shove several fries into her mouth then said, "I was hoping you could help me with my profile."

Rayne reached for her phone. "I think we should take your profile picture right now, with half-chewed fries falling out of your mouth and a spot of ketchup on your cheek."

"Nooo!" Savannah cried, and a mangled piece of french fry fell onto her plate, prompting her and Rayne to burst into a fit of laughter.

Gasping for breath, Savannah reached for her water glass, still giggling, and felt a prickly sensation along her spine. She looked up, and her heart jumped when she saw Colin leaning against the soda counter chatting with the manager. He was once again in well-worn jeans that sat low on his hips and were held in place with a thick black belt. His usual T-shirt had been replaced with an off-white henley in acknowledgment of the unseasonably chilly May evening.

He obviously hadn't seen her, so Savannah watched as he crossed his black-booted ankles in a relaxed pose, although she could see the muscles in his legs and back flexing as he shifted his weight. She suddenly found herself wondering what it would feel like to grip his muscular rear and couldn't stop cataloging the details of his body.

He chatted for a few more minutes then straightened and headed for Savannah's table as if that had been his plan all along.

The moment Colin had walked through the door of the diner, his senses had tingled in a way that he didn't understand until he saw Savannah. He had positioned himself so he could watch her in the mirror behind the soda counter while he talked. He hadn't planned to stop there. He was just walking by and decided to check in with the manager about some business they had together. He saw Savannah notice him about a minute after he got to the counter and had been watching her watch him and clearly enjoying what she saw.

Colin was glad for the confirmation that despite the cold shoulder a few days ago, she was at least a little attracted to him.

When he turned and caught her looking, he didn't even try to hide his smile, especially as he watched that familiar blush creep up her cheeks. Damn, she was cute when she blushed.

"Hey, Red. Hello, Rayne. How are you ladies doing this evening?"

Savannah suddenly didn't know where to look or how to use her tongue, so after an awkward second, Rayne said, "Hi, Colin! Do you want to join us?" and smiled innocently at Savannah's panicked face.

Colin shook his head. "I wouldn't want to intrude on your girl's night."

He leaned a hip against the edge of the booth next to Savannah, and when she inhaled, she could smell him—a mixture of soap and something earthy mixed with a distinctly masculine scent that reminded her of being on top of him in her front yard. She wanted to lean in and breathe him in, but she stayed where she was and refused to even look up at him.

"Any fun plans for the rest of the evening?" Colin asked as he shifted position and brushed his thigh against Savannah's shoulder in a move she suspected was purposeful.

Remembering what she and Rayne had just been talking about, Savannah suddenly found her voice and nearly shouted, "NO! I mean, um, nope. Nothing special. Probably just head home and see what's on Netflix."

"Oh, because I could have sworn I overheard some reference to setting up a dating profile. But that wasn't you two, huh?" Colin asked.

Savannah stared at Rayne, telepathically pleading with her to take the hit on this. To which Rayne telepathically responded, *Not a chance.*

Savannah squared her shoulders and sat up straight in the booth. "Fine. It was me. But so what? Everyone is doing online dating. Especially in this city, where there's no romance, just... interactions."

"Is that a fact?" Colin glanced at Rayne because Savannah still refused to look at him. "Good to know." He stepped away from their table. "Well, I'll let you ladies finish your dinner. Good luck with your project tonight, and you know, if you need a guy's point of view on your profile, I'd be happy to take a look at it."

That earned Colin his first eye contact with Savannah since coming to the table. "Really?" she said, ignoring the tiny stab of disappointment that poked her in the gut.

"Sure. Happy to help," he said with a smile. "You ladies have a great night."

"Bye, Colin!" Rayne called after him as he moved toward the door, but Savannah was silent.

Rayne stared at her until she finally said "What?!" in exasperation.

"You know exactly what!" Rayne said, shaking a french fry at her.

"No, I don't." Savannah reached for her sandwich and immediately dropped it back on the plate.

"You're an insane person. Certifiable." Savannah opened her mouth to reply, but Rayne stopped her. "If you say anything involving the phrase 'The Plan,' I swear to god I will choke you to death with these french fries."

Savannah flopped back in her seat.

"It doesn't matter anyway," she said. "He's obviously not into me."

"If you say so." Rayne took a last noisy slurp of her malted. "Let's get the check and head home. We've got some online profiles to write!"

"Yay! It'll be fun!" Savannah said, even though she suddenly had much less enthusiasm for it than she had just half an hour earlier.

Rayne waved their waiter over and asked for the check.

"You guys are all set," he said. "Colin took care of it for you."

"What?" Savannah and Rayne said at the same time.

"Yup. And…" He turned to look over his shoulder as another waiter came over carrying two clear plastic containers with slices of chocolate cake in them. "He also wanted you to have this dessert to go. He said you were going to need it, whatever that means."

"Who is this guy?" Savannah asked after the waiter had walked away.

Rayne dropped some bills on the table for the tip. "Clearly not someone who is interested in you."

Savannah glared at her and slid out of the booth.

Chapter 7

Two days had passed since the night at the diner, and Savannah couldn't stop thinking about Colin. She finally told herself that it was because she didn't like being in his debt, so on Friday afternoon, when she happened to be walking past Zipped, she decided to go in and see if he was there so she could pay him back.

The restaurant's windows let in a surprising amount of sunlight. The glowing, welcoming interior reminded her of the pub she used to eat at every day when she spent a semester studying in England. During the day, the pub was bright and cheerful and the perfect place for a restorative lunch. In the evening, it transformed into a cozy and lively social hub, dark enough to let your inhibitions down but not so dark that you couldn't see who you were talking to.

She glanced around the room, which was only about half-full of customers, but didn't see Colin. She was about to leave when she heard "Hey there, Red" from just to her left. Turning, she found herself inches from Colin, who was holding an empty plate in one hand and a white rag in the other.

"Here for lunch?" he asked as he moved behind the bar to dump the dish in a black bin.

"No. Actually I came to see you." Savannah followed him to the bar and was rewarded with a wide smile that made his eyes sparkle.

"You know, I had a feeling today was going to be special. Need some help with those dating profiles?" He winked at her as he moved with practiced efficiency behind the bar, clearing plates and refilling drinks.

"Uh...no..." Savannah stuttered.

"Don't tell me you're an afternoon drinker?" he said.

"A what? Oh, no, no." *God Savannah, act like you've been in public before!* she scolded herself. Taking a deep breath, she looked him in the eye. "I wanted to say thank you for buying us dinner the other night."

Colin waved his hand in a dismissive gesture. "The manager owed me. No biggie."

"No, it was really nice of you and really unnecessary...and... uh..." Suddenly Savannah found herself reluctant to undo his gesture by trying to paying him back.

"So you've already had lunch?" Colin asked.

"Well, no, but that's not why—"

"Grab a stool, Red. Take a load off. I'll be right back."

Before Savannah could say anything, he was gone. Just disappearing on him would be rude, and frankly she didn't have anything else to do with her afternoon, so she settled herself on a stool. Colin returned a few minutes later, and Savannah could have sworn she saw a look of relief flash in his eyes.

"How about some iced tea?" he asked as he came up even with her.

"Oh, sure. Thanks." Savannah hadn't planned on ordering anything, but it occurred to her he might get in trouble with his boss if she took up a seat at the bar without eating or drinking anything.

He set the drink down in front of her. "So you were telling me about how it was going with the online dating," he said.

"I definitely wasn't."

"You were definitely just about to start," he said with a wink that made Savannah's stomach do a flip.

There didn't seem to be any way out of this conversation so she said, "There isn't really much to tell. It's only been two days."

"Not going well, huh?" he said with a pitying look.

"Shut up," she snapped, only partly in jest.

The truth was, she had been underwhelmed by the responses she'd gotten so far, and maybe a guy's perspective could help. And since she wasn't interested in dating Colin, she shouldn't have any issue with talking to him about it, right?

"Come on, let's hear it," he said. "I bet I can help."

She sighed, and then she told Colin about the disappointing responses she'd gotten, which ranged from over-muscled/over-testosteroned posturing to illiterate and disturbingly graphic sexual propositions.

When she'd finished, Colin said, "Sounds pretty typical from what I understand. Hey, D!" He called to the waitress with the pink hair that Savannah had seen the last time she was in, and the woman joined them at the bar.

"Diana, Savannah. Savannah, Diana." The women nodded and smiled at each other. "Diana here is something of an online dating veteran," Colin said, and Diana rolled her eyes.

"Sad but true. I've been doing it since before it was trendy. I think I've seen it all," she said with a laugh. "But you aren't doing it, are you?"

"I just started."

"NO! You're young and cute! You do *not* need to be slogging through all the DNA dysfunctions that live online. I bet you can't spit without hitting a guy who'd want to take you out."

"Hardly!" Savannah said with an awkward laugh.

"Come on, D, you've had some good experiences, too, right?" Colin said.

"Some, but they were hard fought. Seriously, sweetie, don't resign yourself to the virtual world before you're sure it's all that's left." Diana patted Savannah's arm before moving away.

"Why are you so quick to give up on real life, Red?"

She paused. "You're going to think I'm crazy. Even Rayne thinks I'm crazy."

Colin leaned in, crossing his arms on the edge of the bar and pinning her down with his magnetic blue eyes. "Try me."

She couldn't resist the kind, attentive look on his face, and next thing she knew, she was telling him all about The Plan, including the type of guy it required.

"Huh," was Colin's only response when she finished.

"Yeah." Normally talking about The Plan made Savannah feel energized and in control. But somehow telling Colin about it made her feel sad.

"How long have you had this plan?" he asked.

She looked down at her lap and twisted a napkin around in her hands. She had no intention of telling Colin about the origins of The Plan.

"Since I was nineteen," she said.

"So it's been a while."

"Yep."

"Well, OK then." He busied himself behind the bar and then seemed to come to a decision. "So here's the problem I see."

"What's that?"

"You're not going to find that kind of guy online. At least not yet. Guys your age aren't online."

"Guys my age?" Savannah said with air quotes. "How much younger than you do you think I am?"

"Five years," Colin said immediately. "But those are a critical five years in a guy's development."

"You're twenty-nine?" Savannah asked. Colin nodded. She had started to hope that he was in his thirties, which would be another reason to not consider dating him. But five years wasn't that big a spread.

"So then where are they—the kind of men I want to meet?" she asked.

"You have to get out and go places. We have a trivia night here on Thursdays. It's pretty popular with dudes whose jobs require suits and IDs on lanyards. There's similar stuff all over the city. Try some of those before retreating into the online world."

"I was planning on finding some meet-ups and joining some young professional groups, too," Savannah said, starting to feel unaccountably irritated by his enthusiasm.

She was pulled out of her thoughts when Diana arrived with a plate of food.

"I didn't order," Savannah objected as Colin set it down in front of her.

"You haven't eaten, right?" He set out a napkin and silverware for her and pulled condiments from farther down the bar.

"Yeah, but—" Savannah didn't want to admit that until she got her first paycheck, which wouldn't be for at least another two weeks, she was on a tight budget. As in "dollar menus" not whatever this amazing-smelling dish was.

"It's a bacon, spinach, and gruyere quiche with fresh tomato slices and parmesan cheese crust," he said. "Take a bite."

She did not need to be enticed. She was hungry, and it smelled better than anything she'd ever eaten in her life. At the first mouthful, she closed her eyes and couldn't suppress a soft moan.

"Like that, huh?" Colin asked, his voice a little rough.

Savannah opened her eyes to look straight into Colin's electric blue ones. "Mmmm hmm," she said as she slid another bite into her mouth and again let her eyes close as she savored the experience.

Colin leaned across the bar and said in a low voice so only she would hear him, "One day, you're going to make those sounds with me, and it won't be from food." And then he disappeared to the back room while Savannah nearly choked on her food.

Colin asked Diana to cover the bar while he took a break. She gave him a long look before agreeing and then headed over to see if Savannah needed the Heimlich.

Colin burst through the back door and into the alley. "You're an idiot! She doesn't want you," he said out loud.

Except he knew that she did—whether she would admit it or not. Chasing a woman wasn't something Colin had ever done. Sure, occasionally they needed a little romancing, a little wooing, which he was always more than willing to do. But this? A gorgeous woman so determined to ignore an obvious connection and attraction? This was uncharted territory.

After a few more minutes of pacing, Colin came to a decision. He was going to win Savannah over if it was the last thing he did. The Plan be damned.

When he went back into the restaurant, he was startled to see a half-eaten quiche but no Savannah. As he stood staring at the empty spot at the bar, Diana came up behind him.

"So what's the deal with her?" she asked as she dumped a stack of plates in a bin.

"What do you mean?" Colin turned away from the empty bar stool and grabbed a rag to help Diana bus the tables.

"I mean, at first she seemed like one of your groupies, but now you're her dating consultant. What's going on?"

"She's different. She doesn't think I'm the right type," Colin said, making air quotes with his fingers.

"If being a bar owner and heir to the largest restaurant conglomerate on the East Coast isn't 'the right type,' then I've definitely been going about this dating thing all wrong," Diana said with a laugh.

"She doesn't know any of that. She thinks I'm just a bartender."

"You mean we've found a woman who didn't immediately fall under your spell? That's a first, huh?"

"It's...something," he said with a shake of his head.

"So when are you going to tell her you're more than a bartender?" Diana asked. "Although the fact that she doesn't want 'just' a bartender is a strike against her in my book."

"I know lots of women who only want me for my family's money or my connections," he said.

"Yeah, your looks have absolutely nothing to do with it," Diana said.

He frowned at her. "Seriously, D. This one time, I'd like to just be Colin, a guy who's had to work his ass off for everything he's got, and not Colin Allison of Allison Inc. She assumes I can't possibly fit into her life plan, but I'm going to prove her wrong. And I'm going to close this deal on my own."

"Oh, this will be fun to watch," Diana said with a chuckle.

Chapter 8

O n Monday morning, Savannah was awake at dawn, as excited about her first day of work as a kid on Christmas. While she stood in the kitchen eating a bagel in her PJs so she wouldn't risk spilling anything on her new suit, she couldn't stop humming.

The door to the basement opened, and Carol walked out dressed in running clothes but looking mostly asleep.

"Good morning!" Savannah said cheerfully. Carol's only response was an angry glare, so Savannah added, "I'm so impressed by your willpower to get up and go running so early every day! I couldn't do it."

Carol grunted as she put in her ear buds. "Well, we can't all be blessed with good metabolisms. Some of us have to drag our asses around the city every damn day just so we can have a carb once in a while." Then she flipped her music on and headed for the front door.

Savannah glanced down at the bagel in her hand and suddenly felt guilty. She grabbed a banana from the counter on her way out of the kitchen, telling herself it balanced out the carbs.

At 9 a.m. sharp, dressed in her new black-and-gray pinstripe suit, white silk blouse, and bright red heels, Savannah sat in the human resources office at the Capitol Foundation filling out paperwork and waiting for her employee training to begin. It was supposed to go until 11 and then she would meet with her supervisor, Sarah, who had recruited Savannah after meeting her at a job fair during grad school. Savannah wasn't sure what else the day would hold, but she couldn't wait to find out.

What the day ended up holding was a lot of overwhelming

information and a lot of new names and faces she was pretty sure she'd forget by the next day. She got lost three times trying to navigate through the warren of cubicles to the bathroom, and she hadn't even tried to find the kitchen on her own yet.

As she flopped down in a seat on the Metro a few minutes past 5, she was exhausted in a way she'd never experienced before, and she kind of loved it. Her excitement had been replaced with a determination to master her new world, and it was invigorating. Her phone beeped, and she pulled it out to see a text message from Rayne.

Still on to spy on happy hour at Zipped tonight?

Savannah had forgotten all about that. After her conversation with Colin, she'd spent some time looking up events and activities she could use to find men. Rayne had been a big fan, pointing out that the networking could be good for her career as well as her love life—which had been Savannah's opening to convince Rayne to do it with her. Rayne's job in media relations for a conservation group on the Hill could definitely benefit from some networking, and her love life could benefit from it even more.

Rayne had reluctantly agreed, but only after making an impassioned speech about how she enjoyed being single and didn't want finding a boyfriend to be her main focus in life. Her one condition was that they show up and observe the events from a distance first, and then if the men all looked super boring, they could cross that event off the list and not have wasted an evening.

When Savannah found a Young Professionals Happy Hour for that Monday at Zipped, it seemed like a perfect place to start because they knew they could at least eat well.

She typed back, *Yep. Could use a drink. LONG day!*

A second later, Rayne's reply popped onto the screen. *My treat to celebrate your first day as a grownup!*

Savannah sent back an emoji of a martini glass followed by clapping hands. Then she slid her phone back in her bag and tried to decompress for the last few minutes of her ride home.

Twenty minutes later, Savannah walked into Zipped looking for Rayne but didn't see her. She was pulling out her phone to check for messages when she noticed Colin waving to her from behind the bar. A smile covered her face before she could stop it, and she headed over.

Colin greeted her with a low whistle. "Lookin' sharp, Red!"

Savannah blushed and avoided eye contact as she arranged herself on her stool and took her suit jacket off.

Colin said, "Are we celebrating your first day, or—" Savannah opened her mouth to answer, but Colin held up a hand to stop her. "Oh, no, wait! Let me guess—the Young Professionals of the Hill happy hour."

Savannah smiled. She'd been a little nervous about coming back in after she'd left last time without saying goodbye so she was relieved to see that he was acting normal tonight.

"Sort of," she said. "Rayne and I are just going to scope it out, and if it doesn't look awful, we'll join in next time."

"By awful, I'm guessing you mean filled with guys you wouldn't want to see naked. Right?"

At the word "naked," Savannah's traitor brain immediately imagined Colin naked, which made her face blush bright red and her stomach do all kinds of acrobatics.

"You are something else, Red," he said, shaking his head and laughing. Then he set out a cocktail napkin and a wine glass and uncorked a bottle of Pinot Grigio.

"I didn't order."

"I told you—I know what you need." Colin paused for a long second before adding, "To drink. But if I'm wrong, I'll make you whatever you want."

White wine was her go-to drink, but she didn't want to give him the satisfaction of telling him he was right. She sat up straight, flipped her hair over her shoulder, and said, "Since you already poured it, I'll drink it. It's fine."

Colin laughed again as he recorked the bottle then moved down the bar to take someone else's order.

Five minutes later, Rayne plopped down on the stool next to Savannah, which was also the last available seat.

"Well, this is the place to be apparently," she said as she hung her bag on one of the hooks under the bar, shrugged out of her blue cardigan, and shoved it into her bag. She was wearing a pale green sundress and flip-flops.

"I know. I almost got into a fight twice trying to save this seat for you."

"Good thing you're bad-ass," Rayne said as Colin walked up and set a cocktail napkin in front of her.

"Hiya, Rayne. How about a vodka tonic?"

"Yes! That's exactly what I was going to order."

"I know," he said with a wink. "I'm just that good." He was talking to Rayne but looking at Savannah, who pretended not to notice though she suddenly felt more lightheaded than her few sips of wine warranted.

"So," Rayne said glancing around the crowded bar. "Which of these young professionals are *the* Young Professionals we're supposed to be checking out?"

Savannah shrugged. "It seems pretty unorganized. No signs or name tags or anything."

Colin set Rayne's drink down on the bar. "Pretty much everyone here is with your group," he said. "Or at least everyone under the age of 40 wearing a suit."

"That doesn't seem like a very good system," Savannah said, wrinkling her nose as she looked around.

"Instead of name tags, they have buttons. But some people wear them on their belt loops or ties or purses. See those guys?" Colin gestured toward two twenty-something men in suits with loosened ties and government ID badges still around their necks. "See the bright green buttons on their ties?"

Savannah and Rayne looked where he was pointing and noticed the buttons for the first time. Glancing around the room again, they realized about ninety percent of the people in the bar had those buttons on.

"At least we have a lot to choose from," Savannah said.

"Probably even more than you realize," Colin said with his eyes on Savannah. When he looked away, he noticed Rayne watching him. Their eyes met, and Rayne raised a questioning eyebrow, but Colin shrugged and went back to his work.

For the next hour, he brought them a series of small servings of appetizers that they didn't order and refused to acknowledge their protests or assertions that they were going to pay for the food. After the third plate, they stopped arguing and just ate whatever he put down.

Savannah nursed her glass of wine for most of that hour, and when she finally took her last sip, Colin was there with the bottle to offer a refill. Savannah put her hand over the glass to stop him.

"Do you want something else?" he asked.

"She's a total lightweight," Rayne said. "More than one drink and it starts to get ugly."

"Hmm, that sounds like a challenge." Colin recorked the bottle and stashed it under the bar.

"Yeah, that's not going to happen," Savannah said as she finished off the last of the brie-and-cranberry crostinis.

"Look at you, hogging the attention of the two prettiest women in the bar. As usual."

Savannah and Rayne both turned toward the sound of a masculine voice and saw a man leaning on the bar next to Rayne. Savannah noted a resemblance to Colin, though this guy was slightly older and taller and had a more rugged look to him.

"Job perk," Colin said, pushing himself back from the bar and reaching for a glass. "Savannah and Rayne, may I introduce my brother Chase."

"Hello, ladies," Chase said, flashing them a magnetic smile. He had the same arresting blue eyes as Colin, though his hair was lighter and he wore it longer and shaggier compared to Colin's closely cropped style. "Do you mind if I ask why, out of all the men in this bar, you're talking to him?" Chase gestured to Colin with his thumb and said "him" like it was something vile.

"Technically, he's talking to us. We're just sitting here," Rayne said as she reached for her third vodka tonic.

"Ah yes, he does have a habit of trapping innocent women into spending time with him."

"Hey!" Colin cried out in protest. "That was a

misunderstanding, and the charges were dropped."

Rayne and Savannah laughed.

"Has he been feeding you food you didn't order and generously refilling your drinks?" Chase asked.

"He's trying to," Savannah said.

"Uh huh. Brother, you need to get some new moves!" Chase leaned across the bar to punch Colin in the shoulder.

"Oh, so then you don't want this gin and tonic I just made you and I should cancel the order of wings Diana put in as soon as you walked through the door?" Colin said to Chase.

"Of course not. But that's called a family perk when—"

"OK!" Colin said loudly as he thunked Chase's drink down on the bar to stop him from saying more. "You wanna go find a seat? Somewhere else?"

Chase gazed at him for a moment then said, "I think I'm fine right here."

"Of course you are," Colin said under his breath as he walked away.

"I'm going to the ladies' room," Savannah whispered to Rayne as she slid down from her chair and made her way across the crowded bar.

Chase looked at Rayne. "Was it something I said?"

"Kind of. Those two are completely into each other but won't admit it—Savannah because she thinks Colin isn't her type, and Colin...well, I'm not exactly sure what's going on with him, but he doesn't seem deterred."

Chase laughed. "No, I'm sure he's not. Colin is everyone's type, but he does enjoy a challenge—not that he has many when it comes to women."

"Well, he'll get his fill with Savannah."

Colin returned a few minutes later with two plates of wings. He set one in front of Chase and one beside Rayne. When she started to protest that they didn't need two servings, Colin said, "He doesn't share well, and I guarantee you'll want some." Rayne shrugged and reached for a wing.

"Where'd Miss Savannah get off to?" Colin asked in what he

hoped was a casual tone. His brother cocked an eyebrow at him, which he ignored.

"She went to the ladies' room, but that was actually a while ago." Rayne craned her head toward the back of the room until she spotted Savannah. "Oh, there she—"

She stopped when she realized that Savannah was talking to a guy with a green button pinned to the belt loop of his suit pants. Colin followed Rayne's gaze.

"Ah. Looks like she's finally doing some networking," Colin said and then got very busy clearing empty plates and glasses from the bar and noisily dumping them into the black bins behind the counter.

"Good for her," he said mostly to himself. "I mean, it's the reason she's here right?"

He stopped moving and looked up to see Rayne and Chase observing his private conversation with amused looks. Colin grabbed a full dish bin and headed to the back.

"Wait—is he jealous?" Chase asked. "So that's what that looks like. Weird."

"Told you he was totally into her."

"Oh boy," Chase shook his head, eyes gleaming. "This should be entertaining."

Savannah had been making her way back from the ladies' room when a young blond man in a gray summer suit and blue tie stepped into her path.

"Hi, I'm Ryan Cleary," he said, holding out a hand.

Caught off guard, Savannah hesitated for a moment before reaching out to shake his hand. "Savannah George," she said with a smile.

Still holding her hand, Ryan pulled her a little closer and leaned in to say, "What's that?"

Savannah put her mouth close to his ear and repeated her name. Leaning back and letting go of her hand, Ryan smiled at her. "Pleased to meet you, Savannah. Are you here with the Young Professionals group?"

"No, but seeing you all here, I think I should be."

"What kind of work do you do?" Ryan asked, leaning close to Savannah's ear when he spoke, although she didn't think it was all that loud in the bar.

"I'm a program manager for a large foundation," she said, liking the way it sounded and making a point to slowly tuck her hair behind her ear in a way that she'd read about in a magazine article titled "Subtle Gestures to Lure Men In."

"Ah, a do-gooder," Ryan said with a half-smile. He gave her a quick once-over and said, "Yeah, I could have predicted. You'll fit right in."

His tone sounded a little condescending, but she told herself she was imagining it.

"I'm a policy analyst at a think tank," Ryan said and then leaned back, as if expecting Savannah to have a big reaction to this information.

"That sounds interesting." In truth, she didn't know what the job entailed despite the fact that "policy analyst" and "think tank" were both on her list of acceptable career fields for potential boyfriends/husbands.

"So what would I need to do if I wanted to join this group?" she asked.

"All you really need is one of these little green buttons." He pointed to the button on his belt loop. "Unfortunately, the gal who hands them out isn't here tonight. But if you come next week, I'll make sure to have one for you."

"Oh great! I think I will come," Savannah said.

"Tell you what, let me give you my card," Ryan said as he reached into the breast pocket of his suit coat, "and if you have any questions between now and then, you can just drop me a line." He smiled as he pressed the card into Savannah's hand.

"Thanks." She glanced down at the card and saw that in addition to his business information, it included a photo of him and a handwritten number labeled "cell."

"Now you give me one of yours, hon. That's how this networking thing works," Ryan said with a chuckle, leaning in closer than necessary and putting his hand lightly on Savannah's elbow. He was making her a little uncomfortable, but she decided to chalk it up to nerves on her part and an odd sense of humor on his part.

"I don't have any on me because I wasn't planning on coming here tonight," Savannah said rather than admit her cards wouldn't be ready until Friday.

"No worries." He reached into his breast pocket again and pulled out his cell phone. "Why don't you give me your number and then I can let you know if anything changes for next week?"

Savannah knew he was just trying to get her number, and although this was exactly what she had set out to do, she found herself reluctant. She glanced toward the bar and felt a pang of disappointment at not seeing Colin—and knew what to do.

"Good idea," she said to Ryan. As she recited her cell number, she congratulated herself on taking the next step in The Plan.

When she got back to her seat, Rayne and Chase were deep in conversation.

"Well, hey there, Miss Popular," Chase teased.

Ignoring him, she said to Rayne, "We're definitely coming next week."

"Is it because of the Ken doll you were talking to?" Chase asked, and Savannah glanced at him, wondering why he seemed so interested.

"No!" she answered a little too forcefully. When he responded with a playful lift of his eyebrow, she said, "Well, not exactly. I mean, we came to check it out and it seems good, so we should participate next time."

"I saw you give him your number," Rayne said.

"I didn't have a card to give him, and he…" Savannah trailed off, suddenly feeling self-conscious about admitting he was flirting with her.

Around a mouthful of wings, Chase said, "I predict he's going to text you within three days and suggest that you meet for a drink. To 'talk about the group' before the next meeting."

Both women turned to look at him. Shrugging, Chase said, "I'm just saying. It's the player's play. And that guy," he pointed to Ryan, "is a player."

Savannah suspected he was right and glanced down at the bar.

"You seem to know a lot about players," Rayne said to Chase. "Takes one to know one?"

Chase laughed and winked at her. "I know a lot things about a lot of things." He pushed himself away from the bar where he'd been leaning and said, "Ladies, it was lovely to meet you both. I hope I will see you again soon." With a tip of an imaginary hat, he strolled out of the restaurant.

Watching him go, Savannah said, "He seems—"

"Really cool?" Rayne interrupted as she gazed after Chase with an almost dreamy look that Savannah had never seen on her before.

"I was going to say different from Colin, but we can go with cool."

A minute later, Diana came up and dropped the bill on the bar between them. As she was gathering their dirty plates, she asked, "Can I get you anything else?"

"I think we're good," Savannah said.

"Great. Have a good night." As Diana turned to leave, Savannah asked, "Where's Colin? We wanted to say goodbye."

Diana looked at Savannah for a second before saying, "His shift ended. He's gone home."

"Oh!" was all Savannah could think to say. She was disappointed, and she couldn't help noticing a chill coming off Diana.

After she left, Rayne looked at the bill and said, "No way all that food and drink only cost twenty bucks!" She dropped two twenties on the bar and slid down from the chair. "He's way too nice. And he's going to go broke if he continues to feeding us like this."

Out on the sidewalk, Rayne looped her arm through Savannah's as they started walking toward home and asked, "So how many boxes did the Ken doll check on your list?"

All the excitement Savannah had felt about Ryan earlier had evaporated, but she wasn't going to admit it, not even to herself. She sighed and said, "About three, so far."

Chapter 9

Jealousy was not a familiar emotion to Colin, and he definitely wasn't a fan. In his experience, most women weren't easily distracted from him, but if they were, he just moved on. He didn't get any masculine pride or rush from competing for a woman's attention or "winning" her away from another guy. Although, now that he thought about it, he hadn't actually faced this situation before. He'd never had such an obvious attraction to a woman who stubbornly refused to acknowledge that she felt it, too. It was usually the opposite—women insisting they had a connection with him that he didn't feel at all.

Not that Colin was a womanizer. When he was with a woman, she had his full and monogamous attention, and he expected the same from her, for however long it lasted. But when it was over, it was over. Easy come, easy go.

Until Savannah had twirled into his life. This woman had him twisted up in a way he'd never experienced. And he was completely unprepared for the gut punch he'd felt when he'd seen her talking to that guy in the bar—a guy who fit into her Plan in all the ways she believed Colin didn't. He'd wanted to grab him by that fancy tie and drag him out of the bar. Instead, he'd left in an attempt to regain his sanity.

He wandered along the waterfront for a while then started walking the fifteen or so blocks back to his apartment. Along the way, Colin made some decisions. He knew in his gut, in a way he couldn't explain or justify, that Savannah was meant to be with him. But he was going to have to let her figure it out on her own. Which meant he was going to have to watch her flirt with—and probably even date—other guys, and he was going to have to keep it together while she did.

The only way she was going to change her notion of what "the right guy" looked like was to date the ones she thought were right and see that they weren't.

Because they weren't him.

When Colin walked into the apartment, Chase was sprawled on the couch in front of the flat-screen TV that took up most of one wall in their small living room.

"What are you watching?" Colin asked as he dropped his keys on the table by the door.

"*Swamp People*, about these families in Louisiana who still hunt alligators for a living. I met some of them when I was down there a few months ago on a shoot. They are a total trip."

Colin walked into the kitchen and grabbed a bottle of beer from the fridge. "How long are you here?" he asked, flopping down on the couch and propping his feet up on the edge of the coffee table.

"No clue."

"As usual," Colin said, taking a long swig of his beer.

"Plans are for suckers, little brother."

"Amen to that, brother." Colin reached out and clinked his bottle with Chase's.

They watched TV and drank their beers in companionable silence for several minutes before Chase said, "So what's the story with your friends from the bar earlier?"

"Which friends?" Colin asked.

"Come on. That cute dark-haired chick with the hippie name...Storm?"

"Rayne," Colin corrected.

"Right. And her friend...uh...Georgia?"

"Savannah. How do you get as much play as you do when you can never remember anyone's name?"

"Because every girl answers to Sunshine," Chase said with a grin, holding out his bottle for a supporting clink, which Colin refused to acknowledge.

"Anyway," Chase said, dropping his bottle back to his thigh. "So what's the deal with you and this Savannah? You hit that and then she decided she could do better? Again?"

"You're such an ass," Colin said, but his tone was light. "There's no deal with me and Savannah. She just moved to the neighborhood. We barely know each other."

He got up and went into the kitchen, where he tossed out his bottle and pulled two more from the fridge. "Why is there never anything to eat in this apartment?"

"Liar," Chase called from the living room. "I saw it all over your face. Especially when she was talking to that douche in the suit. This chick has got you all twisted up."

"I'm not twisted up," Colin said, restlessly opening and closing cabinets. "Why don't we ever go grocery shopping?"

"Because I live here about 10 days a year and you spend at twelve hours a day at restaurants where we can eat for free."

"This isn't how adults live. Adults have more than just beer and coffee in their fridge."

"Do they, Mr. Cranky Pants? Did you read that in your *Being an Adult for Dummies* book?"

"Screw you," Colin said as he threw himself into the armchair to the left of the couch and handed Chase a beer. They continued to watch groups of men hunt alligators in swamps for a few minutes until something occurred to Colin.

"Did you just refer to Rayne as 'cute'?"

"I did," Chase said, wiggling his eyebrows at Colin as he took a sip of beer.

"She's not your type."

"All women are my type. Plus, she can actually carry on an intelligent conversation, which, although not a requirement, is a nice change of pace."

"She's Savannah's best friend, and...she's just not that type of girl, OK?"

"By 'that type of girl' you mean the type who would be interested in me?"

"I have no doubt she'd be plenty interested in you. But you'll do that thing where you make her fall for you and then you'll take off to your next job, which just so happens to be in the last remaining corner of the universe that doesn't have cell service, and you'll end up staying for three months and she'll end up heartbroken and sadly asking me if I've heard from you every time I see her."

"That is not what I do."

Colin snorted and took a long pull from his beer.

Chase sighed and said, "Fine. But it's not like I do it on purpose. I'm always upfront about my lifestyle, and nothing happens without their full consent. I can't help it if they all think they'll be the one I'll want to hang around for."

"Stay away from Rayne, Chase."

Chase grunted in response, which Colin chose to take as agreement.

The next day at work, Savannah sat in her cubicle learning her way around the internal network and going through the files of the programs she would be working on, trying to get oriented. She was supposed to meet with her supervisor Sarah that afternoon to go over any questions, but so far Savannah only had one question, and it was "Huh?"

For the third time in the last twenty minutes, she leaned back in her chair, closed her eyes, and did a cleansing yoga breath to regain her focus. A focus that kept wandering from her files to Colin's blue eyes and wondering if he'd seen her talking to Ryan. And if it had bothered him at all. Not that it mattered.

"Argh! Focus, Savannah, focus!" she scolded herself under her breath.

"What's that?" Sarah's head popped around the opening of Savannah's cube. "Did you say something?"

"No!" Savannah said a little louder than she'd intended. "Nope, just talking to myself. A bad habit I have when I'm concentrating." She hoped that sounded reassuring and not like Sarah had hired a crazy person.

"No worries! I know there's a lot to take in with all those files," Sarah said. "Maybe just focus on getting to know the ones with reviews coming up next month. You can find the schedule on our shared calendar."

"Great idea!" Savannah plastered a big smile on her face to

stop herself from saying she wasn't sure she could remember how to access the shared calendar.

For the next two hours, she managed to focus at least eighty percent of her brain on her work, devoting a scant twenty percent of her mental energy to thinking about the way the color of Colin's eyes changed slightly depending on his mood. Her concentration was finally broken by her stomach rumbling at noon.

She stood up from her desk and stretched her hands over her head to work out the kinks in her back. When her phone dinged with an incoming text message, she dropped her arms and took a second to stifle the butterflies that set loose in her stomach at the idea that the message could be from Colin.

"He doesn't even have your number, fool!" she muttered as she rummaged in her bag for her phone. She was only mildly surprised when she read, *Hi Savannah, it's Ryan from last night. Just wanted to say it was great to meet you!*

She sighed and dropped the phone back into her bag. She hated those types of texts—vague and with no clear indication of what he wanted. If he wanted to ask her out, he should just say so, instead of playing this game, where she has to write back *Yea, me too!* and then wait for his next message, which would hopefully include an active verb. She could reply with an invitation to get together, but she didn't like starting out having to do all the work.

When she glanced across the sea of cubicles to the windows and saw that it was a beautiful sunny day, she made the executive decision to take her lunch outside and deal with Ryan later.

Exiting her office onto the busy downtown thoroughfare of Connecticut Avenue, she turned north toward Dupont Circle and eventually found a low wall to sit on amid the other office escapees, dog walkers, homeless people, and nannies out for some sun with their charges. She popped open her Tupperware container and settled in to do some people watching while she ate her salad.

After twenty minutes, she picked up her phone and reread Ryan's text, and remembered Chase predicting he'd wait three days to contact her. Savannah figured the fact that he'd texted her the next day meant he wasn't the player Chase pegged him to be. And since it would be counterproductive to ignore his text at this point, she hit reply and typed, *Hi Ryan. Thanks! It was great to meet you too.*

Three minutes passed before her phone dinged with a response.

Would you want to meet me for a drink or something tomorrow night?

Savannah smiled. At least he got there quickly.

Sure! Where?

Zipped again? @7?

Um, kind of tired of that place. How about somewhere else?

Five minutes later, when Ryan hadn't responded, Savannah stood and put her empty container back in her bag.

"Something tells me Ryan doesn't know anywhere but Zipped," she murmured to herself as she slung her bag over her shoulder and began to slowly walk back to her office. As she passed Starbucks, she decided to treat herself to one of her guilty pleasures—a mocha latte. While she was standing in line, her phone dinged, and she pulled it out to see that Ryan had finally responded.

How about The Lounge on C Street right by the market?

Savannah had passed by that place, and it looked pretty nice. Ryan was quickly redeeming himself from the initial lame text.

Savannah typed, *Sounds great. See you tomorrow at 7.*

As she walked back to her office sipping her latte, Savannah felt a small seed of anticipation about her date.

The next phase of The Plan was in motion.

The afternoon flew by in a blur of reports and statistics and shared calendars. At the end of the day, as Savannah stood pressed between hundreds of other commuters on the Metro train heading home, she realized that she'd been so busy all afternoon she hadn't thought about Colin or Ryan or even checked her personal email for new matches or updates about networking events. It felt good to be totally focused on work. As she was contemplating a quiet night spent in her PJs with some reality TV, her phone beeped with a message from Rayne.

Is tonight the trivia night at Zipped?

Savannah sighed and typed, *That's Thursdays.*

A moment later, Rayne replied, *Oh. Is there anything going on there tonight?*

Savannah suspected Rayne's sudden interest in Zipped might be connected to trying to play matchmaker with her and Colin, and she had no interest in going along. So she wrote back *Dunno. Don't care. Need a night IN. Please?*

Several minutes passed without a response from Rayne, so Savannah typed, *PLEASSEE?*

Can we get Chinese?

Savannah smiled and typed, *YES. My treat!*

She couldn't believe how relieved and excited she was at the idea of a night in with Rayne. She'd been so focused on getting her life set up for the past month that she felt like she'd been working two jobs.

At 10 p.m., Rayne and Savannah were in the living room with half-empty Chinese takeout containers and two empty bottles of wine on the floor and a *Project Runway* marathon on TV. They were painting each other's toenails when Carol walked in.

"Carol!" Rayne called, waving her hands above her head.

"Having a girls' night in?" Carol asked in a tone that Savannah thought could be either snarky or amused.

"We are! You should join us! We...uh..." Rayne hesitated as she picked up both empty wine bottles. "OK, there's no more wine, but we have some fortune cookies. And we'll paint your nails!"

"Tempting, but I'll pass. I have a very important date with my bed that I don't want to be late for." Savannah decided that this was Carol being friendly, which was something new and interesting.

"You're just getting home," Rayne said as a statement more than a question, making a point of looking Carol up and down through narrowed eyes. "You were on a date!" Rayne shouted. "Sit! Tell us EVERYTHING."

Carol laughed but still managed to sound a little sad. "I was definitely *not* on a date. Just a work dinner with some donors."

Turning to Savannah, Rayne said, "Carol is a bigwig over at the Smithsonian."

"If by bigwig you mean the person who has to be first in and last out and go out to dinner with boring old men, then I guess I am," she said.

"So definitely not a date?" Rayne asked, looking disappointed.

"Not a date. Never a date. I'm past that. Dating is for young women—like you two."

Savannah and Rayne responded with cries of "NO!" and "You're not old!" to which Carol laughed and waved them goodnight before going down to her basement bedroom.

"Speaking of dates," Savannah said, "let's hurry and finish our toes, so we can go pick out an outfit for tomorrow!"

"Yes," Rayne said as she quickly dabbed bright pink polish on Savannah's toenails. "I'm feeling all kinds of inspired by *Project Runway*."

Chapter 10

The next night, at 7:00 on the dot, Savannah stood on the sidewalk in front of The Lounge. Like most businesses in the Eastern Market area, it looked like a charming converted row house. She and Rayne had decided to go with an outfit that could transition from work to evening so Savannah wouldn't have to stop at home in between. She was wearing a navy blue pencil skirt with tiny gray dots, navy heels with a white bow just above where her pink toes peeped out, and a sleeveless white silk blouse. Her hair was pulled up into a high ponytail to show off the chunky red necklace that matched her bracelet. She'd left her suit jacket at the office and had a soft gray cardigan in her bag in case the restaurant was cold.

Taking a deep breath to calm the butterflies in her stomach, she walked up the steps. Just as she reached for the door, it swung open to reveal a young woman dressed in a starched white shirt, black bowtie, and black apron covering what Savannah assumed was a skirt over her black tights.

"Welcome to The Lounge," the woman said with a warm smile while stepping back to usher Savannah in.

"Oh! Thank you," Savannah said as she crossed the threshold into a small atrium with a hostess stand and stained-glass doors opening off either side.

"Do you have a reservation?" the woman asked as she led Savannah to the hostess stand, where another, almost identical woman was holding a tablet.

"I'm not sure. I'm meeting someone. Ryan Cleary?"

"Oh yes. He's already arrived. Right this way please."

Savannah followed the second woman through the doors on the left, then through a dimly lit bar and lounge filled with heavy oak, brass, and dark leather, and through another stained-glass door into an amazingly beautiful room whose walls seemed to be made mostly of glass. The floor was slate, there were plants in every corner, and the tables were an eclectic mix of brightly painted wood and metal, as if assembled from yard sales. And yet the effect was elegant and fun instead of messy and chaotic.

The hostess led Savannah to a table in the back corner near a small pond.

Ryan rose to his feet as she approached. "Savannah! I was starting to wonder if you were going to stand me up!" he said with a little laugh.

"Oh! Am I late?" She looked down at her watch and saw that it was just two minutes past seven.

"You know what they say: On time is actually late. Early is the respectful option."

"Really? That's a thing?" Savannah said as she reached for a chair across from him.

"Oh, don't sit way over there." Ryan leaned over to pull out the chair to his immediate left. "It will be hard to hear each other from all the way across the table. Sit next to me."

A small voice in Savannah's head told her to stay where she was, but then she reminded herself that she had to be all in on these dates if this was going to work. With a smile that felt a little forced, she sat down next to Ryan and noted that at least here she had a better view of the garden and pond.

"So let's get you caught up, hmmm?" Ryan motioned with his drink to the waitress, who came right over holding a small electronic tablet instead of a notepad. "You probably like those feminine fruity drinks, right?" He glanced at Savannah but continued without waiting for a response, "Let's get her a vodka and cranberry."

The waitress glanced at Savannah for approval, and although Savannah knew that drink was too much for her, especially on an empty stomach, she didn't want to be rude, so she nodded to the waitress.

"Would you like to see a menu?" the waitress asked, speaking more to Savannah than Ryan. "We have some great appetizers and specials tonight."

Savannah started to say yes just as Ryan said, "No, thanks."

Startled, she glanced at Ryan, who looked at her for a moment as if deciding something. Then he smiled and said, "Oh, what the heck." To the waitress, he said, "Go ahead and bring a menu over, sweetheart. Thanks," as if it had been his idea all along.

So many things were odd about that interaction, but Savannah didn't have a chance to process any of it before the waitress set down a menu and Savannah's drink next to it.

"A toast!" Ryan said, holding up his glass. Savannah smiled and lifted her glass as well. "To meeting new people and having some fun." Ryan wiggled his eyebrows as he clinked his glass with Savannah's. Taking a small sip before setting her glass down, she reached for the menu, but Ryan put his hand over hers. "Slow down there, darlin'. Why don't we chat for a bit and see if this is even going to be worth the cost of appetizers?"

Savannah bit back a sarcastic remark about how charming he was and instead said with a smile, "Sure. Fair enough."

Ryan sat back in his chair, swirling the ice in his tumbler. "So I think you said you're a do-gooder, right? Nonprofit or something?"

"Yes," Savannah said, crossing her right leg over her left and turning her body slightly away from Ryan. "I'm a program manager at the Capitol Foundation. We give out grants to dozens of nonprofits each year in the area of poverty and urban renewal."

"Huh. Any money in that kind of work?"

Savannah's mouth opened and closed a couple of times before she found a polite response. "Well, generally nonprofits aren't where you work if you want to be rich. But it pays the bills."

"Sure, and you get that warm and fuzzy feeling all day, right?"

"Exactly," Savannah said with a big smile, hoping that would end the conversation. She took a deep swallow of her drink. "So tell me more about what you do."

"Oh, you know, just your average mid-level D.C. paper pusher," he said, leaning back in his chair and looking pleased with himself. "My outfit looks at economic trends and makes predictions about where the next booms and busts will be, where big companies and the government should focus their investments, that sort of thing."

"That sounds like interesting work," Savannah said, although in truth it sounded incredibly dull.

"Well, it definitely does more than just pay the bills," Ryan said with a wink. He leaned forward and looked at Savannah a little too closely. "You know, you should wear your hair down."

"Oh, um. I...do sometimes" she stammered, feeling uncomfortable.

"I know. You had it down when we met. It looked much better. You look kind of uptight with it all pulled back like that. Not really the right energy for a date, don't you think?"

Savannah was flustered, but she had no intention of taking her hair down just because he wanted her to. "Well, maybe later. I'd need to go to the ladies' room to brush it out."

"Something to look forward to then," he said with a smile that made Savannah feel a little icky.

For something to do, she took another sip of her drink and felt it burn as soon as it hit her empty stomach. Setting her drink down, she reached for the appetizer menu again.

"Oh, I see! Maybe if I buy you some food, you'll take your hair down, is that it?" he said with another chuckle.

"No, I'm happy to pay for the appetizers. I'm just really hungry."

"I thought you girls always ate before your dates," he said.

"I guess I didn't get that memo."

Ryan laughed like she'd said something hilarious, but her patience was rapidly eroding.

"That's a good one," he said, patting her knee. "You're funny."

Savannah brushed his hand away and picked up the menu just as their waitress approached the table.

"Do you have any questions about the menu?" she asked.

"No, we can read just fine, doll," Ryan said, rolling his eyes at Savannah before pulling the menu out of her hands. Savannah looked up the waitress and tried to wordlessly communicate an apology. The waitress smiled calmly and watched Ryan.

Without looking up, Ryan said, "We'll take the meat and cheese plate. And I could use a refresher." He held up his glass.

"And for you?" the waitress asked Savannah.

"No, we're sharing it," Ryan said, putting his arm across the back of Savannah's chair, which made her lean forward.

"Well, it's meant for individuals, so it's a little small to share."

"For 8 dollars?! No, we'll be just fine with one. Thank you."

The waitress nodded, gave Savannah a sympathetic glance, and left the table.

"So where were we?" Ryan asked, his arm still around Savannah's chair.

"Um, you were telling me about your job," she said trying to slide as far forward as possible without falling out of the chair.

"I think we were talking about when you were going to take your hair down," he said and wrapped a strand of her ponytail around his finger.

"No, I don't think we were." She was starting to wish she'd planned an exit strategy with Rayne. Then she felt his finger trail down her neck and immediately jerked away.

"Jumpy, jumpy," he said. He pulled his arm away from the chair only to place his hand on her knee. "You need to relax. Maybe I can help with that."

Savannah shoved his hand off her knee and got to her feet.

"Look, Ryan, I don't think we're on the same page here. I'm going to go."

"Whoa, whoa, whoa!" he said holding up his hands. "I'm sorry! I'll behave. Please. Seriously. I overstepped and I see that now. I won't do it again."

Savannah remained standing as she debated what to do. The sudden shift in his demeanor was a little off-putting, but this was closer to the guy she'd met at Zipped.

"Look. I'm just nervous," he said. "You're so pretty and smart, and I was intimidated and...I thought females liked take-charge guys so I was trying to—"

"I think your first problem is assuming that all of us 'females' are the same. Why don't you just be you and I'll just be me and we'll see where that gets us?"

"That sounds just crazy enough to work," Ryan said with a gentle smile, and Savannah relaxed a bit.

Shifting the chair a few more inches away from him, she slowly sat down and said, "Let's start over."

"Great! OK." Ryan cleared his throat. "Savannah! Good to see you again. You look very nice."

Smiling, Savannah said, "Thank you, Ryan. It's nice to see you, too."

The food came, and Ryan quickly ordered a second plate after admitting that it was too small for them to share. And for the next half-hour, the conversation was pleasant and Ryan resembled a relatively normal, although dull, guy.

As Savannah took the last sip of her drink, she glanced at her watch. They'd been there almost an hour, which seemed like sufficient time to say she'd given it a real chance. But she was having trouble concentrating on the conversation because her mind kept drifting to the fluffy slippers and sweat pants waiting for her at home.

Ryan saw Savannah glance at her watch and said, "Should I get the check?"

Relieved that he also seemed to sense the lack of a connection, Savannah smiled. "Sure."

When the check arrived, she reached for her purse, but Ryan said, "I've got this."

"I'd be happy to split it," she said, digging in her bag for her wallet.

"Nonsense. But tell you what, you can get it next time, if that'll make you feel better," he said.

Savannah knew there wasn't going to be a next time, but this didn't seem the moment to discuss it.

Ryan handed his credit card to the waitress, who swiped it through the tablet she was holding and turned it toward him to sign with his finger.

"Fancy!" Ryan said as he scribbled a line across the screen.

"OK," he said downing the last of his third drink. "Shall we?"

He stood and motioned for Savannah to precede him through the restaurant.

Out on the sidewalk, he came up next to her and threw his arm around her shoulder. "Where to next, sweetheart?"

"Oh! I, uh, need to call it a night. I have to get up early."

"Come on! The night is young. We've still got plenty to learn about each other." He slid his hand down her bare arm and pulled her tightly against him.

"Ryan! Please let go," Savannah said, trying not to panic even as all the alarm bells that had been softly ringing earlier in the evening got louder.

"But you're supposed to get the next round. That was the deal." He loosened his grip and ran his hand up her arm back to her shoulder, and Savannah took the opportunity to step back.

"I never said the next round would be tonight," she said with a forced laugh.

Anger flashed across Ryan's face before he got control and tried to be charming again. "Come on, don't be like this." He stepped closer, and she stepped back until she was up against the side of the restaurant's stairs. "Let's go somewhere else, someplace less fancy where I won't be as uptight. I'll even buy you dinner if that will help."

"No. Thank you, Ryan. I really need to get home." She tried to move to her right to get out from between Ryan and the stairs, but her blouse caught on something so she stopped.

"Come on." He stepped closer until his chest brushed against hers. His boozy breath was hot against Savannah's face, and she suddenly she felt like she was in a Lifetime movie. "I never even got to see this gorgeous hair out of its tie," he said in a low voice as he wound his hand around her ponytail.

Savannah went ice cold. She wondered why no one walking by was helping her, then she realized they probably looked like a couple being romantic.

"Get away from me, Ryan, or I'll scream," she said.

"You know, I figured you for a screamer," he said, and she felt his heavy, hot breath on her face.

He outweighed her by at least eighty pounds, but she dropped her bag and pressed her hands against his chest to try to push him away anyway.

"That's better," he said, giving her ponytail a tug that was hard enough to hurt.

"Get. Off. Me. NOW!" Savannah yelled through clenched teeth, while trying again to slide between him and the staircase.

"Everything OK over here?" a male voice asked.

"We're fine!" Ryan yelled without moving a muscle.

"No, we're NOT!" Savannah shouted, still trying harder to push him back.

"Hey, buddy, why don't you give the lady some room?"

Savannah turned her head toward the voice and saw an older man who was definitely big enough to take Ryan.

"Let go of me! Get off me!" Savannah yelled and squirmed with everything she had, and suddenly she was free and Ryan was several feet from her, having been pulled off by her good Samaritan.

"Why don't you mind your own business?" Ryan said, stumbling drunkenly as he tried to straighten his jacket.

Savannah crouched down to pick up the contents of her bag, which had scattered when she dropped it, but she was shaking so bad that it was slow work. The doors of the restaurant opened, and the hostess came down the steps to help her.

"Are you OK?" the hostess asked.

"I'm fine!" Savannah said.

Then she looked up and saw that a small crowd had started to form. Ryan was drunkenly yelling at the man and whoever else caught his eye about lying women and quid pro quo.

"Oh god, everyone is staring." Savannah buried her face in her hands.

"I'll take care of it," the woman said.

Savannah kept her head down and focused on gathering her stuff, but she noticed that a busboy had come down the stairs and was standing near her as well.

"Sir, I'm going to have to ask you to leave this area immediately," the woman said.

"Fuck you! It's a free country. I can do whatever I want."

"Sir, you are in fact on private property. We own this patio area in front of the restaurant. And you are drunk and disorderly. If you do not quiet down and move along in the next three seconds, I will call the police."

"Screw you, you dumb bitch!"

Without another word, the woman pulled her phone out and dialed. "Yes, I want to report a drunk and disorderly on the property of The Lounge," she said and paused a moment as she listened. "Yes, thank you."

She lowered the phone and took a step toward Ryan. "It's our lucky day. There's an officer a couple blocks away. He'll be here in just a minute."

Ryan seemed to be considering his options and then turned to hail a passing cab.

"Good choice," the hostess said as he pulled open the door.

"Fuck you," Ryan replied as he slid into the cab.

Savannah slowly rose to her feet but remained behind the busboy, embarrassed by the crowd of onlookers.

The hostess turned to the crowd. "Hey, folks. I'm sorry for the disturbance. Everyone is welcome to come inside for a drink on the house."

The crowd cheered, and a handful of people headed toward the restaurant door while others continued on their way. Savannah hurriedly pulled her bag over her shoulder and moved away from the stairs.

"You're sure you're all right?" the hostess asked. "I didn't really call the police just now, but I could if you think you want to press charges."

"No, I'm fine. Just embarrassed. Thank you so much, and I'm so sorry for the trouble."

"You have absolutely nothing to apologize for. By the way, I'm Jessica," she said, holding out a hand.

"I'm Savannah," she said with a smile as she took Jessica's hand. Something about her was calming in a familiar way, but Savannah couldn't place it.

"I hope you'll come back soon under better circumstances,"

Jessica said with a warm smile.

"Thanks. I will."

As Savannah started to walk away, Jessica called out, "Oh, wait!" and Savannah turned back to face her. "I'm afraid your pretty blouse is ripped!" She reached out to touch the tear that went down the length of the shirt, revealing Savannah's bra strap and most of her right side.

Savannah sighed and opened her bag. "Of course it is," she murmured as she pulled out her cardigan.

Jessica held Savannah's bag while she put her sweater on. When she was done, Jessica said, "You can't even tell."

Savannah gave her a tired smiled and turned toward home, suddenly feeling more drained than she could ever remember feeling.

Chapter 11

As she turned the corner onto her street, she saw Sweet Happens all lit up and beckoning to her like the coziest, safest place on earth. Veering off toward the glowing shop, Savannah pulled open the door and was enveloped in a rich smell of chocolate and sugar and knew that she would find something here that would make everything OK.

"Hiya," the woman called cheerfully from behind the counter. "You are just in time. I was about to close up."

"Can I still get something?" Savannah asked, panic in her voice.

The woman looked at her a little more closely before saying, "You can have anything you want. It was a slow day so we still have lots to choose from."

As Savannah peered into the glass-fronted case, the woman asked, "Are you a chocolate girl?" Savannah nodded. "I thought so. How would you like a cup of old-fashioned hot chocolate? I was just making some for myself."

"I'd love some," Savannah said, and it felt like the truest statement she'd made in days.

"Great! You pick out a treat while I get it for you."

The woman bustled off with more energy than Savannah would have expected from someone who'd presumably been working since early that morning. She decided it must come from being surrounded by all those heavenly treats and briefly wondered if she'd picked the wrong career path.

By the time the woman came back with a sturdy paper cup filled with steaming hot chocolate and piled high with whipped cream, Savannah had decided on a chocolate cupcake with raspberry buttercream frosting.

"Excellent choice," the woman said as she put the treat in

a plastic cupcake-shaped container and rang up the sale. "Hot chocolate's on the house, the cupcake is three dollars." Savannah pulled some ones out of her wallet and handed them over.

"Thank you. You're a lifesaver," she said.

"Bad date?"

"The worst! How did you know?"

"That's the main reason I started staying open later on weeknights," she said with a laugh as she started wiping down the counters. "You wouldn't believe the business I get from women on their way home from bad dates."

Somehow knowing she wasn't unique made Savannah feel a little bit better. "Mind if I sit on the patio to eat this?" she asked.

"Go for it. It'll be at least half an hour before I get to putting the chairs away. I'm Crystal, by the way."

"I'm Savannah. And your shop is definitely the best part of this neighborhood."

Crystal beamed. "Thanks! Don't forget to tell your friends."

As Savannah sat outside sipping her hot chocolate and nibbling at her cupcake, she started berating herself for letting things get so out of hand tonight.

"I'm such an idiot," she said out loud.

"Talking to yourself, Red?"

Savannah snapped her head up at the sound of Colin's voice and felt her stomach flip over in that way it always did around him. He was smiling as he headed toward her. She wiped a stray tear from her cheek and pulled her hair loose from its messy ponytail.

"Having a little dessert?" His smile faltered as he got a closer look at Savannah's face. "You OK?"

"I'm fine." She reached for her hot chocolate but then pulled her hand back when she realized it was trembling.

Colin sat down next to her. "Savannah, tell me what's wrong," he said, and somehow hearing him use her name instead of a nickname made tears well up.

Looking into his warm eyes, lit up by the light spilling from the bakery window, she fought the urge to tell him everything and said, "It's nothing. Just a bad night."

"Bad date?" he guessed.

Savannah laughed. "God, am I that much of a cliché?"

"How bad?" he asked.

"Oh, nothing that left any marks, other than on my ego," she said, trying to sound light.

"Please tell me what happened." Colin was close enough that she could feel his body heat and smell what was quickly becoming a familiar scent of...him. But unlike when Ryan had been this close, now Savannah didn't feel threatened. In fact, she felt utterly safe.

She hesitated a moment longer then recounted the evening as briefly as she could, including how impressed she was with the way the hostess had handled Ryan.

"She was amazing. I felt like such a weak, stupid girl. I let him get me cornered. I let him bully me. I should have left after the first five minutes—"

"Hey, hey, hey, give yourself a break."

"No! I don't deserve a break." Savannah stood up and paced across the patio. "I'm too nice! I'm too trusting! I have no survival skills." Spinning to face him, she said, "I had no idea how I was going to get away. If that guy hadn't come over—"

Suddenly she couldn't stop shaking, and tears were rolling down her face. Colin closed the distance between them in two long strides and pulled her into a hug.

"Shhh, you're safe now. Everything is OK," he murmured into her hair.

Savannah relaxed into him but didn't allow herself to hug him back because she knew she would lose what little emotional control she had. After a few seconds, she took a deep breath and pulled away.

"I'm sorry. I'm OK now," she said with a smile and a quick swipe at her eyes. She had stopped shaking, and Colin looked impressed at how quickly she had pulled herself together.

"New plan," he said, clenching and unclenching his fist and looking like he wanted to punch something. Savannah had a brief, thrilling image of him knocking Ryan right on his ass.

"You'll have all your dates at my bar," Colin said.

Savannah stared at him. "What? No, I—"

"Because you're planning to continue going on dates with virtual strangers, right?"

"In a manner of speaking. I mean, I can't let one guy derail—"

"Right," Colin said cutting her off. "So you'll schedule any future first dates at Zipped, where I can watch your back."

Savannah thought about it and had to admit that it did sound like a good plan. And if he was suggesting it, then clearly he had no interest in her himself, which was good, despite the way her stomach dropped at the thought. His face was serious and concerned, and she fought the urge to step back into his arms.

"OK," she said softly.

"OK?" Colin repeated, sounding a little surprised. "You promise you'll have all your first dates at my bar?"

Savannah nodded. She noticed that he kept referring to Zipped as "his bar." Maybe he took his work more seriously than she thought.

"Great." Colin let out a breath, and she walked back to the table to pack up what remained of her cupcake and retrieve the hot chocolate.

"I'm going to head home," she said. "I'm wiped."

"I'll walk you."

"It's just a couple blocks," Savannah protested, although secretly she was glad she didn't have to say goodnight to him yet.

"I'm walking you home, Red. Deal with it." As he took a step toward her, Crystal came out onto the patio.

"Hey, Colin! Fancy seeing you here," she said in a way that made Savannah think it wasn't random that Colin had come by.

"Hey, Crystal!" To Savannah, Colin said, "Give me one second. And don't even think about leaving without me." He stared at her until she nodded agreement. When he walked over to Crystal, she told herself she didn't care what his business was with her.

She wasn't trying to eavesdrop, but even so, she heard him say, "So, um, everything OK here today?" and was surprised at the tension that had crept into his voice.

"Yeah," Crystal said, "but even though it was a slow day, I've got a bunch of custom orders to do tonight, and I'm not sure I'm going to be able to make it all the way to tomorrow night on my own."

"I'll stop by in the morning around 6 and see how you're doing, and I can get you a boost if need be. Does that work?"

"Sounds good, babe," Crystal said with a smile. Then she started dragging chairs from the patio and stacking them against the wall.

A boost? Savannah had no idea what that was about, but her curiosity was definitely piqued. Colin was at her side within seconds. "Ready?" he asked, and Savannah could sense a definite urgency to leave. After a beat, she decided it was none of her business, and they headed toward her house.

They walked in companionable silence for a few steps before Savannah said, "Maybe I should take up kickboxing."

"Kickboxing?" Colin repeated.

"For self-defense. So next time I'll have some options."

They reached the sidewalk in front of her house, and Colin put his hand on her arm. "Learn kickboxing or whatever other self-defense skills you want, Red, but just know that most guys aren't like that, OK? Most of us are regular old nice guys who know how to take no for an answer."

Savannah turned to face him in the moonlight and tried not to think about how romantic the moment felt. "Even ones with tattoos and two-day-old scruff?" she teased.

Colin let out a slow breath before saying, "Especially us."

Savannah grinned back at him and knew that if he took even the smallest step toward her, she was likely to kiss him.

But instead, he took a step back, hands firmly shoved in his pockets. Savannah felt the distance like a slap.

"Get inside," he said softly. "It's late."

Savannah nodded and walked up the path to the porch. At the door, she turned around to find Colin in exactly the same spot.

"Just making sure you get inside OK," he said.

She started to make a joke about the likelihood of something happening between the steps and the door but bit it back, wanting instead to enjoy the feeling of him watching over her. She slid her keys into the lock and pushed the door open. When she turned to shut it, she smiled. Colin was still standing in the exact same spot.

Savannah ran straight up the stairs to Rayne's room. Not seeing any light under the door, she knocked softly before entering the room and stage-whispering, "Rayney? Are you sleeping?"

The bedside lamp snapped on, and Rayne said, "How was your date?"

Savannah set the cupcake and hot chocolate on the dresser and flung herself onto Rayne's bed. "I've had the weirdest night."

She filled Rayne in on everything with Ryan and then Colin's plan, which Rayne endorsed fully. But Savannah didn't mention the walk home or the strange moment she had shared with Colin out on the sidewalk. She wanted to keep that to herself.

Chapter 12

The next day Colin could not stop thinking about the state Savannah had been in when he ran into her at Sweet Happens, and by early afternoon, he'd started to wonder whether she might not have told him the whole truth about her date. He seethed to think about that douchebag Ryan physically hurting her.

After the lunch rush, he pulled out his cell phone and called his older sister, Jessica.

"Hey, stranger," she said as a greeting.

"I just saw you, like, two weeks ago at one of Mom's cocktail parties," he protested.

"You live *and* work within five blocks of me, and yet I have to go to Georgetown to see my baby brother?"

"This is why I prefer texting."

"Oh, fine. What's up?"

"I heard you had a little excitement at the restaurant last night," he said, cradling his phone against his ear as a he rang up a credit card sale.

He could hear her sigh through the phone. "Facebook's got nothing on the restaurant industry," she said. "How did you hear about it already? And technically it took place outside the restaurant."

"I know the woman who was involved. I ran into her afterward, and she told me the story."

"How's she doing?" Jessica asked, sounding genuinely concerned. "She seemed pretty rattled when she left. Not that I blame her."

He nearly dropped the customer's credit card in the bin of dirty dishes behind the bar. "Was it bad?" he asked, unable to keep the concern out of his voice.

"Bad enough," Jessica said. "The guy was a real creep."

Colin felt the tension in his gut. "She insisted she was OK, but I wanted to get your take on it."

"Trying to decide what level of knight in shining armor to deploy, huh?"

Colin smiled at how well his sister knew him. "Something like that," he said with a chuckle. "The guy's a regular here, which is how she met him, so I feel a little responsible. I'm trying to decide if I ban him, or just throw him or throw him up against a wall next time he comes in."

"Go with the wall," she said. "But you have nothing to feel bad about. If anyone does, it's me. We kept serving him even when he was clearly drunk, and their waitress said he was a bully and an ass at the table. We should have done... something."

Jessica told him what had happened, and her version pretty much lined up with what Savannah had said, which made him feel marginally better.

"How many free drinks did you end up giving out?" he asked.

"About a dozen, but almost all of them also bought food, and several people mentioned us positively on Facebook and Twitter, so all in all, not a bad night for us."

"Sounds like you handled it well. Have you told Dad?"

"I sent him an email this morning but no reply yet. I don't think he'll fuss too much. Although if you wanted to screw up something big today as a distraction, I would let you."

Their dad was obsessive about the image of his properties, especially top-tier ones like The Lounge, and when it came to the restaurants his kids worked in, he had even higher expectations.

"Better idea," Colin said. "Tell Mom Chase is in town. She'll freak out that she had to hear it from you, and Dad will be so busy trying to calm her down and track Chase down and get him out to the house that we could probably burn down an entire restaurant and he wouldn't notice."

"Excellent idea!" Jessica said with a laugh. "I've gotta run, but tell your friend that I'm sorry again and that if she wants to come back, I'll buy her dinner."

Chapter 13

Savannah's fourth day of work was no less overwhelming than the previous three had been. She was still trying to get up to speed on the programs she was overseeing and still got lost on her way to the kitchen.

But today had the added bonus of her first staff meeting, which meant that all the executives and managers from Development, Communications, Administration, and Finance were there. From her department, it was Savannah, Sarah, and two other program managers, both of whom had been at the Capitol Foundation for at least two years. During the meeting, Savannah learned that the person she replaced had been well loved, and most people seemed to doubt that Savannah would be half as well liked or competent. She even overheard the CFO ask why an intern was in the management meeting, gesturing dismissively to her.

Instead of getting upset, she resolved to do whatever it took to prove herself. Right after the meeting, she had gone straight to Sarah's office and asked to be put in charge of the annual donor appreciation reception, which was only a month away but an excellent opportunity for Savannah to demonstrate her talents. Her predecessor had worked at the foundation for a year before taking over the event, but Savannah didn't want to wait that long.

After Savannah made her case, Sarah agreed but made her promise to ask for help the minute she needed it.

Savannah decided to get off to a running start by staying late to go over the files from the previous years' events and make a list of all the things she needed to do.

At 5:30, her phone dinged with a message from Rayne. *Trivia night at Zipped tonight?*

Savannah typed, *Working late. Too much to learn!*

Oh come on! It's your first week. And we said we were going to go to meet men.

Since when is that such a priority for you? We can go next week.

Several minutes passed before Rayne's reply came. *I'm kind of hoping to run into Colin's brother again* followed by a blushing-face emoji.

Savannah laughed out loud. Chase must have made quite an impression on Rayne. She looked at the stack of files and her rapidly filling-up notepad and then back at Rayne's text. She finally decided that if she worked for another hour, then reviewed her notes on the Metro, and maybe brought a folder home to look at before bed, she could make it work.

She picked up her phone and typed, *Fine! See you there at 7:00.*

Rayne's response was an immediate *I LOVE YOU.*

Savannah had been so focused on work during the metro ride that she hadn't thought ahead to what it would be like to walk into Zipped. As she pulled open the door and the sounds of a lively happy hour washed over her, she felt two conflicting emotions bubble up inside her. One was a stab of fear that Ryan would be there. Not that she feared for her safety, but she didn't want to deal with him. The other was a little tingle of anticipation at seeing Colin.

Savannah slowly made her way to the bar while scanning the room for Rayne. When a woman got up from a stool, Savannah grabbed it and hopped on, hooking her bag under the bar while continuing to glance around.

"Well, look who it is!" Colin said with a grin as he appeared in front of her and slapped down a cocktail napkin. "Looking for Rayne?"

"Yes. She's the one who insisted we do trivia night here."

"Aw, man, and here I thought you'd come to see me."

"Oh! No, I just meant, I was going to stay at work, but of course seeing you is a bonus." As soon as the words left Savannah's mouth, she felt herself blushing and wished she could hit the "undo" button.

"I'll take it," Colin said with a heart stopping grin that made his blue eyes twinkle.

Savannah busied herself by looking at her phone to see if Rayne had texted her.

"Rayne is here, by the way."

Savannah looked up. "She is? Where?"

Colin tilted his head to the far end of the bar. Savannah looked in that direction but didn't see her. "I don't—"

Suddenly a muscular back shifted sideways, and Savannah realized it belonged to Chase. Rayne sat facing him, more starry-eyed and giggly than Savannah had ever seen her.

"Oh!" Savannah said. "Well."

"Yeah." Colin winced when Rayne laughed at something Chase said. "I told him to stay away from her, but clearly he's hard of hearing."

"Why? What's wrong with Rayne?" Savannah was instantly on the offensive. She sat up straight and flipped her hair behind her shoulder.

Colin chuckled as he watched her assume her fighting stance. "Stand down, Red. Rayne is great. But my brother…well, let's just say she can do better."

"Oh, really? They seem to be having a good time." Savannah watched as Rayne said something that made Chase throw his head back and let out a hoot of laughter.

"Everyone has a good time with Chase. Until he's gone." Savannah gave Colin a questioning look. "He travels for work. A lot. Usually leaves without much—or any—warning. Never really clear when he's coming back. Somehow never has cell service, that kind of thing."

"Ahhh, I see. That's not going to work for Rayne. She's not a casual fling kind of girl. She likes stability in her life. And she doesn't play games."

"I figured as much," Colin said, setting down a class of ginger ale with a cherry in it. "Seeing as how she's your best friend."

Savannah glanced at the drink.

"Just ginger ale," he said. "I figured you might not be up for drinking tonight. But I can add a splash of Jack if you want."

"No, this is perfect. Again." Savannah took a sip and marveled at how he really did always know the perfect drink.

"I'm going to bring you out some of the happy hour apps, too," he said, rapidly stabbing icons on the register's monitor.

Savannah knew she should protest because if the pattern held, he wasn't going to charge her much, if anything, but at the same time it felt nice to have someone else make decisions and fuss over her. Especially when that someone was a sexy man with tattoos poking out of his T-shirt that she grew more curious to explore every time she caught a glimpse.

As she waited for Colin to return, she watched Rayne, who still hadn't noticed that Savannah was there, and began to dread having to tell her about Chase. It had been a very long time since Rayne had shown so much interest in a guy. Too bad it was the wrong type. Again.

Colin returned a few minutes later with a plate piled with small triangles of grilled-cheese sandwiches and another plate of french fries.

"Three different takes on a grilled cheese sandwich and, of course fries because obviously," he said with a grin.

"Obviously," Savannah said, returning his grin.

"Trivia is about to start. Were you going to play?" he glanced at Rayne, who was clearly not going to be a good teammate.

"Nope, I'm just going to eat my comfort food and then try to drag Rayne out of here."

"Sounds like a plan." Colin picked up a remote and flipped the channels of the TV behind the bar and the screen that hung behind the small stage set up near the bay window. The screens lit up with a graphic that said, "Welcome to Trivia Night!" and a woman jumped on the stage and grabbed the mic.

As the woman started going over the rules, Savannah glanced down the bar at Rayne, who seemed to be coming back to earth because she was looking around. Their eyes met, and Savannah waved and smiled. Rayne looked a little sheepish, but when Savannah smiled an *It's OK* smile, Rayne smiled back.

With just her eyes and facial expressions, Rayne said, *Can you believe it?* cutting her eyes at Chase, who was watching the first trivia question appear on the screen.

Savannah responded with *Uh huh!* in a similarly nonverbal manner than only best friends can pull off.

Rayne silently asked, *Is this OK?*

Savannah gave a wave of her hand and made a face that said, *No worries.*

Rayne smiled gratefully and returned her attention to Chase.

For the next hour, Savannah nibbled on food and kept one eye on Rayne and one eye on the trivia questions. Colin moved around the bar waiting on people, but whenever he had a spare minute, he would wander back to Savannah and they would try to guess the answers or make fun of each other's wrong answers.

When the host announced that they were going to take a fifteen-minute break, Savannah decided it was her cue to leave. She hadn't slept much the previous night, and it was starting to catch up with her. The next time Colin came by, she told him she was going to head out, expecting him to argue. Instead he said, "Yeah, you look exhausted. I'm actually surprised you lasted this long."

"Aren't you a sweet talker?" Savannah said, thinking about how fun it had been hanging out with him tonight. She had enjoyed the easy back and forth they'd established. Maybe they really could just be friends.

"I try," he said with a wink. "Are you going to take Rayne with you?"

"That's the plan," Savannah said. At some point in the last hour, Rayne and Chase had moved from the bar to one of the secluded booths in the far back. Savannah looked at Colin. "I'm not going to walk back there and find something X-rated going on, am I?"

Colin chuckled. "I make no promises. But I will go back with you, and if necessary, I'll hold Chase back while you grab Rayne and run."

"Please be joking," Savannah muttered as she slid off the stool and threw her bag over her shoulder.

"Has she been drinking?" Savannah asked as she met up with Colin at the end of the bar.

"Yep."

"Awesome."

When they reached the table, Savannah was relieved to see that although they were snuggled in on the same side of the booth, nothing graphic seemed to be happening.

"Hi, Rayne!" Savannah said loudly to get her attention.

"Savannah! Hiiiii!" Rayne cried cheerfully, stretching her hands toward her across Chase's chest.

"Hi, sweetie," Savannah said. "We need to go home now."

"Already?" Rayne said, looking disappointed.

Chase looked up at Savannah with a smile and said, "I'd be happy to walk her home later, if you need to go." He still had his arm around Rayne's shoulder and reached for his drink with his other hand.

"That's nice of you, but we both have to get up early," Savannah said. "And, Rayney, I haven't seen you all evening and I wanted to tell you about the big project I got assigned at work."

"What big project?" Colin asked, and Savannah was embarrassed because she'd just been using it as an excuse to get Rayne to move more than two inches from Chase.

"Oh, it's the big donor appreciation event next month," she said. "I talked my boss into letting me be in charge of it. It means a ton of work, but if I pull it off, I might even get a promotion out of it."

"That's great, sweetie!" Rayne said. Then she nudged Chase to let her out of the booth. "I want to hear all about it."

Chase slid out of the booth then helped Rayne out and handed her purse to her.

"Thanks for keeping me company tonight. I had a great time," he said, sounding, at least to Savannah, like he was sincere.

"Me, too," Rayne said with a giggle. "Bye." She gave a little wave and let Savannah steer her toward the door. "Oh wait, I didn't give him my number!" Rayne tried to turn back, but Savannah kept her arm around her and kept her heading straight for the door.

"I'm sure he knows how to find you."

As soon as Rayne and Savannah were gone, Chase said, "Since when are you in the C-blocking business, bro?"

Colin glared at him. "You can have any other girl in this city, but you had to go straight for her? I told you to stay away."

"*She* started talking to *me* tonight."

"You moved it to canoodling in the back booth."

"She's hot! And smart and funny as hell," Chase said. "And who put you in charge of deciding who she can date?"

"She's not your type. She likes stability and reliability. All the things you hate."

Chase rolled his eyes. "I don't *hate* stability. You're so dramatic." Colin crossed his arms and stared at him until Chase said, "Hate is such a strong word."

Colin started to move toward the kitchen, and Chase said, "At least I'm honest about who I am."

Colin stopped and turned to look at him. "What the hell is that supposed to mean?"

"Face it, bro," Chase said. "That girl is messing with your head. You can't even be honest with her about who you are."

"You don't know what you're talking about."

"Diana told me about your scheme to pretend to be a lowly bartender until your girl falls head over heels and then the pumpkin turns into a carriage and you slide the glass slipper on her foot—"

"Go home, Chase," Colin said.

"Fine. But don't say I didn't warn you."

"I won't—because I don't intend to have this conversation with you again. Now get the hell out of my bar," Colin said, but there was more weariness than heat behind his words.

On the walk home, Savannah realized that Rayne wasn't as drunk as she thought, she was mostly just giddy about Chase.

"We're basically in the same line of work," Rayne said. "He takes pictures of nature, and I try to preserve nature so that he can keep taking pictures. It's perfect!"

"Sweetie, did Chase happen to mention that he travels a lot so he can take those pictures?"

"Yeah, he said he travels a fair amount, but it's up to him whether he goes or not."

"That's not how Colin made it sound. In fact, Colin thinks you should steer clear of Chase. He said he's a bit...unreliable."

Rayne was quiet for a moment. She finally pushed a stray strand of hair away from her face and said, "I should have known. Why are the unreliable ones always so attractive?"

"Probably because they can get away with it," Savannah said. She wished more than anything that she could have told her friend to go for it.

Linking her arm through Rayne's, she sighed. "God. Men suck."

"Mm-hmm," Rayne said, and they walked the rest of the way home in silence.

Chapter 14

Saturday morning was another gorgeous spring day, and Savannah woke up at 7:30 feeling energetic and optimistic about her life. She jumped out of bed and grabbed her laptop then crept quietly down the stairs. In the kitchen she moved on tiptoes so as not to wake Carol as she made a pot of coffee and helped herself to a donut from the box that had appeared on the counter overnight.

Balancing her mug of coffee, laptop, and donut, she made her way out to the front porch and settled in to see if she could line up at least one date for the next week. She'd taken a little break from it after the Ryan incident, but The Plan wasn't going to fulfill itself. On Friday, Sarah had told Savannah that she was impressed by how hard she was working and how quickly she was picking things up and offering great insights. Savannah had been relieved to get that reinforcement. So with the career part of her plan seeming to be on track, it was time to get back to the dating side.

After logging into her "It's Just Drinks!" account, she found several messages waiting for her from men who wanted to meet for drinks. After eliminating the obviously unsuitable ones, she was left with three options. She sent each of them a message asking if they were available to meet next week. Having all her dates at Zipped definitely made her feel more comfortable, but it also provided some scheduling challenges. She wasn't going to go in on a Monday again because of the Young Professionals group, and Thursday night trivia was too crazy to be a good first-date environment. And then it hit her that she had no way of knowing whether Colin would even be working at a time she might schedule a date.

Opening a new browser window, Savannah brought up

Facebook and typed "Colin" into the search field. Shaking her head at herself, she realized she didn't even know his last name, which felt strange given how often she'd pictured him naked. There were several Colins in D.C., and eventually she found a semi-public profile of a Colin Allison with a photo of a guy standing with the sun behind him so his features were in darkness, but he had "bartender" as his occupation and was friends with a Chase Allison and Crystal from Sweet Happens.

Taking a deep breath, she sent him a friend request then went back to her dating site to look for some more suitable men. Less than two minutes later, a notification popped up on her Facebook page. Colin had accepted her friend request.

Clicking on the messenger icon, she typed, *Hey! I'm assuming this is the Colin who's the bartender at Zipped?*

His reply was almost immediate. *I knew it was just a matter of time before you started stalking me, Red.*

Smiling, Savannah typed, *I'm not stalking you! I just realized that I didn't have a way to contact you to coordinate my dates with your schedule.*

I'm always working. But just in case, here's my cell number. You can text me to confirm if you want.

Savannah wondered if she should give him her cell number, too, but before she could decide, another message popped up. *Maybe you should give me yours so I'll know it's you...and not one of my other stalkers.*

So you have a lot of women checking your work schedule? Savannah teased, although now that she'd mentioned it, she was curious how many women were in his life. Not that it mattered, of course.

Why? Jealous?

Savannah blushed at being busted.

No! She stopped typing, trying to think of something flip or snappy to write back but couldn't think of anything. Finally she typed, *Besides, it's none of my business.*

A long pause followed before Colin's response came through. *There's no one else keeping track of my schedule, Red. Just so you know.*

Savannah's stomach did a full acrobatic roll, and she couldn't keep the smile off her face. Then she flashed to his cryptic conversation with Crystal last week and reminded herself that she didn't really know him that well, despite how it felt at times.

Well, like I said, it's none of my business. But I will give you my cell number so you'll know it's me.

I'll take what I can get, Colin replied, followed by a winky emoji.

A few minutes later, one of the guys Savannah had emailed replied and suggested that they meet that evening for a drink. Savannah felt slightly disoriented shifting from chatting with (and thinking about) Colin to talking to a stranger, but she reminded herself of her goal and told the guy she could meet him at Zipped at 7:00.

Going back to Facebook messenger, she typed, *First drinks date tonight! 7pm.*

Colin immediately responded. *I'm not working tonight!*

But you just said you're always there! Savannah's mind whirled as she tried to think of how she'd explain to her date that she needed to reschedule.

Gotcha! Get there by 6:45 so we can decide on a bail-out signal.

You're not as funny as you think.

Yes, I am. See you tonight.

Savannah picked up her nearly empty coffee mug, feeling a sense of anticipation building in her. But she didn't know if it was for her date or for seeing Colin.

Colin couldn't suppress his smile as he shoved his phone back in his pocket and reached for the door at Sweet Happens.

"I was wondering when you were going to put that phone down and come in here," Crystal said as she shoved a tray of hot donuts into the display case.

"Just finishing up some business." He was still smiling when he reached over the counter to help himself to one of the to-go cups.

"Must have been some good business to give you that stupid grin." Crystal's voice was light, but Colin knew she was looking for information.

"Probably won't amount to anything more than a bunch of trouble," he said over his shoulder as he filled the coffee cup at the machine by the counter.

"Speaking of trouble, how's that brother of yours?" Crystal refused to meet Colin's eye as she spoke, focusing instead on putting donuts into a bag for him.

"Hey! I told you—if you're going to talk about Chase, our deal is off."

"I'm just making conversation!"

Colin cocked his head and stared at her until she glanced up then away with a blush.

"Fine." Crystal tossed the pastry bag at him. "But he doesn't have to avoid me. I'm not going to freak out on him if he walks in here."

"What did I just say?! One more strike and you can find another source. I'm risking my neck here keeping you supplied."

"Fine!" Crystal's eyes darted to the door, which was still closed tight. "I won't mention you-know-who ever again."

"Then we're good." Colin smiled and pushed through the door and out onto the empty patio, where his thoughts immediately returned to Savannah. He knew he shouldn't be excited that she was coming to Zipped on a date, but as he'd just told her, he'd take what he could get.

At 6:45 on the dot, Savannah walked into the bar. She'd gone with a more casual look than her previous date and was wearing dark-wash jeans, high-heeled sandals, and a flowy short-sleeved pink blouse over a white lacy tank top. Her brown hair was loose around her shoulders, and she'd put on minimal make-up.

When Colin saw her, he let out an appreciative whistle, and Savannah rolled her eyes even as she blushed.

He came out from behind the bar and said, "So I was thinking you should sit in the window seat." He placed his hand lightly on the small of her back and guided her toward the bay window. She was suddenly caught up in his touch and his smell—that delicious combination of soap and masculinity with a hit of something sweet. "This way, you can sit across from him, and you can look out the window if he's boring but also have a sight line to me in case you need anything. OK?"

It took Savannah a second to realize that Colin was waiting for a response. "Yes! Yeah. Sounds good."

Colin studied her for a minute before saying, "Sure you're up for this?"

"Yes! Just normal first-date jitters," Savannah said with a laugh as she quickly sat down in the chair he had indicated to put some space between them.

"Let's have a signal in case you need an exit strategy," he said.

"What if I give you a hand signal and you call my phone with an emergency?"

"Ugh. That's so cliché. How about, you place an order for catfish nuggets, and then the server will let me know, and I'll rescue you?" Colin had come up with the idea earlier but was hoping it sounded spontaneous.

"What will you do?"

"I don't know," Colin said with a smile. "We'll see what the moment calls for."

"This sounds complicated."

"It'll be fun. The key to dating a lot is to make it fun. Otherwise, your soul will get crushed after the third bad date."

"What if the date is good?" Savannah asked playfully. "What if this is The One?"

"Odds are definitely against you, Red," Colin said with a wink, hoping like hell that he was right.

Safely back behind the bar, Colin took a deep breath and tried to clear his head. When she'd come in wearing jeans that looked custom cut for her curves and her hair all soft around her face, he'd had a primal urge to grab her and lay the kind of kiss on her that would have marked her as his for everyone to see. While he was showing her to her table, he'd been so distracted by the fruity scent surrounding her that if she hadn't sat down when she did he would have nuzzled his nose against her neck.

Out of the corner of his eye, he watched her sitting at the table, nervously running her hands through her hair and fidgeting with her phone, and he knew that if this plan was going to work, he couldn't sit here and watch her on these dates.

He saw Diana going into the kitchen and followed her. He had explained his plan to her earlier, and she had expressed disapproval. Now he told her about the catfish nuggets code, and her role in it didn't help.

"Why can't you just get a normal girlfriend?" she asked.

"It's a solid plan."

"Just keep telling yourself that."

Colin was starting to have second thoughts, but he wasn't going to admit it or change his strategy. "Are you gonna help or not, D?"

With a sigh, she said, "Of course I am. You sign the paychecks."

"That's my girl," Colin said with a laugh. "I've got some work to do in my office, so if she needs me, just come get me."

"Hiding, huh?" Diana said as she headed back out into the restaurant. "Yeah, you've clearly got this under control."

Twenty-five minutes after Peter sat down across from Savannah, she was ready to order catfish nuggets.

"Do you mind if we get something to eat?" she asked when Peter stopped talking long enough to take a breath. Who knew someone could have that much to say about life insurance?

"Oh, boy, ordering food," he said. "That means this is going well, right?"

Savannah smiled noncommittally. Glancing up, she caught Diana's eye, who nodded but took her time making her way to the table.

"Another glass of wine?" she asked, and Savannah wondered if she knew the code.

"Definitely, but also, um, are you still serving catfish nuggets?" Savannah asked, looking Diana in the eye.

Without any reaction, Diana said, "We sure are. I'll get those right out to you."

Savannah worried briefly that she was going to have to actually eat catfish nuggets. Whatever those were.

Two minutes later, Colin came out from the back and walked toward their table. "Savannah! I didn't know you were coming in today, sweetheart! What a nice surprise." As he reached the table, he turned as if just noticing Peter. "Who's this, honey? Someone from work?"

Savannah was caught off guard and didn't know what to say, eventually stuttering out, "Um, he's, uh, my…"

Colin turned to Peter and held out his hand. "You must be Jason. Pleased to meet you!"

Peter's face paled, and he said, "Um, no. I'm Peter." He glanced from Colin to Savannah with a question on his face.

"He's…Colin…I mean, I, uh…" Savannah continued stuttering.

"Am I seeing this right? Did you bring another man into my restaurant just to rub my nose in it? I agreed to try this open relationship thing your hippie friends were raving about, but this is too much."

Colin made a good show of looking angry, but Savannah could see the humor in his eyes.

"I, uh… thought you were off tonight. Honey." Savannah was slowly starting to get on script.

"I'll just bet you did." Colin crossed his arms and turned to face Peter. "And now you've gone and dragged this nice man into our drama." He narrowed his eyes. "Or maybe you're into this open relationship thing, too? Huh?"

Then Colin's expression softened. He looked Peter up and down and said, "Hmmmm. I might be able to get on board with that."

"No! No. No," Peter said, jumping up and knocking his chair back. "I'm not…that's not…I've got to go." He fumbled in his pocket and threw some crumpled bills on the table before carefully sliding past Colin.

As the door swung shut, Colin dropped into the seat Peter had vacated and looked at Savannah for a split second before they both burst out laughing.

"What the hell was that?!" Savannah asked as she wiped tears from her eyes.

"It worked, didn't it?"

"You're insane. Poor Peter."

"Eh," Colin waved his hand dismissively. "Come on over to

the bar and tell me what was so bad about Peter, and I'll get you some actual food."

After she had settled herself at the bar, Savannah asked, "Why are you so focused on feeding me?"

"Well, it works with stray cats." He set a glass of white wine on the bar in front of her.

"Huh?"

"To keep them coming back." Colin winked at her as he moved down the bar to put in her food order and then immediately went to bus a few tables so Savannah couldn't respond. Which was fine because she had no idea *how* to respond.

Over the next two weeks, Savannah had five more dates at Zipped, and they all ended with her ordering catfish nuggets and some variation on the same scene with Colin, but with Savannah getting better at playing her role. After the third date, Rayne started coming to the restaurant to watch the scene play out—and to try to run into Chase. But he had apparently left town on a photo assignment shortly after trivia night.

Now as Savannah assumed her spot at the table in the window for her sixth blind date, Rayne settled herself at the bar. Colin set a gin and tonic in front of her, and she said, "So what's it going to be tonight? The open-relationship routine—or maybe the long-lost lovers?"

"How do you know we'll need a routine tonight?" Colin said. "This could be the one that sticks."

Rayne shot him a look that he refused to acknowledge. "The odds favor dinner theater as the likely outcome," she said.

"I guess we'll see." Colin smiled and quickly moved down the bar to check on some other customers.

By the time he made it back to Rayne's end of the bar, Savannah's date had arrived and they seemed to be having a good conversation.

"So how's all this been for you?" Rayne asked, gesturing with her head toward Savannah's table.

"It's been a lot of fun," Colin said with a smile, though he wouldn't meet her eye. "I took this improv class a couple years ago, so it's been fun to finally put it to use. Plus, I think it's helping Savannah keep her spirits up with all these bad dates."

Colin knew he was rambling and forced himself to stop. The truth was that it had been way more of an emotional roller coaster than he'd been prepared for. He started each date with the usual excitement about seeing Savannah, then resisted the urge to touch her, then waited anxiously hoping she ordered catfish nuggets while also hoping she didn't because playing these scenarios with her—reading each other so easily, laughing and dishing about the guy's flaws afterward—was torture. A sweet, delicious torture that Colin both savored and dreaded.

He had originally seen this as a way to keep her safe while giving him time to show her how these other guys couldn't measure up to him. But now he was starting to worry that he'd miscalculated and that each order of catfish nuggets just pushed him deeper into the friend zone. But as much as he hated watching her with these other guys, what he hated even more was the idea that eventually she wouldn't order the nuggets, and he'd have to watch her walk out with another guy.

Suddenly he became aware of Rayne staring at him and realized he'd gotten lost in his thoughts, but he couldn't remember what he'd been saying.

With a soft laugh, Rayne said, "So this is all no big deal for you then?"

Colin laughed, too, and said, "Yeah, piece of cake," before heading back to hide in his office.

Diana intercepted him before he reached the door. "You're on," she said with the disapproving tone she used anytime Savannah was involved.

"That was fast." Colin looked toward the window and saw Savannah gripping her wine glass with a fake smile on her lips. He headed for the table, deciding to go with the long-lost lover routine.

As her date slid out the door, Rayne slid into the chair across from Savannah and shot a pointed look at Colin, making him head for the bar without a word.

"What are the chances," Rayne asked gently, "that you're purposely picking the wrong guys just to be able to play this game with Colin?"

"Zero," Savannah said, but she shifted uncomfortably in her seat. The guys were good on paper—that wasn't the issue. But what *might* be the issue was that she wasn't giving them half a chance because as soon as she saw Colin, her focus was destroyed. But she wasn't going to admit that to Rayne.

"This one lasted almost an hour," Savannah said by way of defending herself.

"So what happened to suddenly bring on the catfish nuggets?"

"He told me he lived with his mom."

"Well, it *is* expensive to live—"

"By choice. He said she's his best friend and that it felt weird to be out doing something social without her."

"OK, that was a legit catfish date."

"Thank you. Now let's go see what Colin feeds us tonight," she said as she got up from the table.

"Wait." Rayne reached out and grabbed Savannah's wrist, and Savannah slowly sank back into her chair.

"I'm serious," Rayne said. "I think you should consider throwing The Plan out the window or at least putting it on hold for a few years."

"No! I'm not doing that."

"I know. And that's why I'm staging this intervention. If you're sure you want to stick to The Plan and just be friends with Colin, then having your dates here isn't going to work."

Savannah opened her mouth to protest and was surprised at how upset she got at the idea of this ending.

"Unless!" Rayne said before Savannah could gather words. "Unless you agree to seriously give these dates a chance. And that means no more catfish nuggets. The whole point of having the dates here was so that you'd be safe from aggressive assholes, right?"

Savannah nodded.

"So you don't need an entire improv scene every time a guy

is boring or a mama's boy. You have to start enduring these dates and getting out of them on your own, just like every other woman in this city."

Savannah still felt a little panicked at the idea of ending catfish nuggets, but it was better than not coming into Zipped at all.

After staring out the window for a few minutes, she said, "There was this one guy, a few nights ago. Steve. He wasn't bad. I actually didn't even have to catfish nuggets him because he got a call about work and had to go. I assumed he was ditching me, but he's been emailing me to set up a second date."

"That's great! A second date! You should totally do that. But maybe not here?"

Savannah sighed. "He emailed me yesterday to ask if I wanted to go to this lecture at the National Geographic museum tomorrow night. It sounded kind of interesting."

"Perfect! Why don't you email him back right now and say you'll go?" Rayne pushed Savannah's phone toward her.

Picking it up, Savannah shot Rayne a look. "I thought you didn't support The Plan. Why are doing this?"

"Because, sweetie, I support *you*. And this is what you want, so I'm going to help you get it. That's all."

With a smile, Savannah brought up her email on her phone, accepted Steve's invitation, and gave him her cell number.

"Good girl!" Rayne said. "Now we can eat."

As they dug into bowls of ratatouille and chunks of crusty brown bread smeared with butter, Colin said, "So what's the date schedule for next week, Red? I'm thinking of changing up the routine a bit. I think the regulars are starting to get a little bored." He winked at Rayne, who shook her head, not wanting to encourage this game.

"Um, I'm actually going on a second date tomorrow," Savannah said, surprised at how hard it was to say.

Surprise flashed briefly on Colin's face. "How do you do a second date after catfish nuggets? You been having first dates behind my back, Red?" he said, trying to sound playful.

"No. Remember that one date last week who ditched me?

Well, he emailed the next day and confirmed it really was a work emergency and we've been emailing a bit, and so we're, um, going to a lecture at a museum tomorrow night."

"A lecture at a museum, huh? Sounds thrilling." Colin hated how bitter he sounded, but he couldn't help it. "Well, just so you know, catfish nuggets aren't available for delivery." He turned and stalked back to the kitchen.

"That went well, I think," Rayne said.

Ten minutes later, Diana came over and asked if they needed anything else. When they said no, Diana said, "OK, then you have a good evening," as she dropped a check on the counter.

Savannah picked it up, and her heart sank when she saw that for the first time ever, it was for the full amount of their bill.

"Do you think he's mad at me?" she whispered.

"He's just mad at losing his performance slot," Rayne said. "Or maybe his boss finally got after him about giving away all these free meals."

She took the slip from Savannah and pulled some money from her wallet, which she left on the counter with the bill.

"Come on, babe," she said, sliding her arm through Savannah's. "Let's go find something for you to wear on your museum date tomorrow."

Chapter 15

The next night, when Savannah got out of the Uber she'd taken home from her date, she found Rayne and Carol sitting on the porch, a bottle of wine between them.

"Wow, Mom and Dad, you didn't need to wait up," Savannah said as she climbed the steps to the porch.

"I wasn't waiting for anything," Carol said. "I was just stopping this one from drinking alone."

"I, on the other hand," Rayne said, gesturing with her wine glass, "was definitely waiting up. How'd it go?"

Savannah leaned against the railing and said, "It was fine. It was nice."

Rayne raised an eyebrow, and Carol made a "harrumph" noise.

"No, seriously. Steve is a good guy. He's smart and courteous and interested in my work, and he's funny. In his own way. But he definitely has a sense of humor. He's definitely checking all of the boxes."

"What about chemistry?" Rayne asked.

"Yeah, chemistry! From what I remember that's kind of important!" Carol chimed in, and Savannah wondered if she might be a little drunk.

"There's chemistry. He kissed me tonight. It was actually pretty romantic. We got coffee after the lecture and then we came out onto the street and he insisted on getting me an Uber instead of a cab, and then as it pulled up, he kind of grabbed me and kissed me." Savannah smiled as she recalled the scene.

"Did you kiss him back?" Carol asked.

Blushing, Savannah said, "I did. And we're going out again later this week."

She had honestly enjoyed the kiss and was looking forward to seeing Steve again, but that also made her feel a little guilty, like she was cheating on Colin. Which was ridiculous. She noticed Rayne watching her and wondered if she could read her mind.

"Well, good," Rayne said after a minute. "It sounds like it's going great."

"Yep. Well, I'm pretty tired. I'm going to head to bed. You kids stay out of trouble," she said as she pulled open the door.

"I don't even know what trouble looks like!" Carol called after her.

Yup. Definitely drunk.

It had been more than a week since Savannah had seen Colin, although he'd "liked" a couple of her posts on Facebook and started following her on Instagram so she guessed he didn't completely hate her. She'd gone on her third date with Steve, which had also been nice, and he had kissed her a little longer at the end of the night, and that had been nice, too.

The next day, Savannah sat on the patio of Sweet Happens with a double latte and scone enjoying a lazy Sunday afternoon, wondering if things with Steve would ever get better than "nice." Or if she even wanted things to go beyond "nice."

"Well, look who it is!" came a familiar voice behind her. Even if she hadn't recognized it, the way her stomach flipped was all it took for her to know that Colin was there.

"Hey, yourself," she said turning around and smiling at the sight of him in jeans that were worn down in all the right places, with a gray-and-black graphic tee and that smile that made her tingle in places that Steve's smile definitely didn't.

"I was sure you'd have starved to death by now since you haven't been by the bar in a while." He pulled out a chair and sat down across from her, looking completely at ease.

"There's this place that Rayne discovered—called a grocery store?" Savannah said.

"Those places are total rackets. Not only do you have to pay for the food, but then you have to cook it. Neither of which is the case at my bar," he said with a smile.

"We were starting to worry that we'd overstayed our welcome.

And we figured you were going to get in trouble with your boss for giving away all that food."

He looked away for a second. "Don't worry about my boss," he finally said. "That last bill was a misunderstanding between me and Diana. I was going to explain next time you came in, but you haven't been around."

Savannah couldn't be sure, but Colin seemed a little nervous.

"No! Of course we'll pay for our food! That's not why we go there."

Her voice trailed off, and she blushed a bright pink as she realized that the reason she went there was sitting across from her, eyebrow cocked as he waited for her to finish, knowing exactly what she was avoiding saying.

Savannah cleared her throat and reached for her latte to give her something to do other than watch Colin's sexy mouth twitch in amusement. After taking a slow sip, she realized that he was not going to do anything to ease the awkwardness of the moment. So she cleared her throat, narrowed her eyes at him in playful annoyance and acknowledgment of the moment, then flipped her hair over her shoulder and sat up straighter.

"So, yeah, I haven't been avoiding you because you made us pay for dinner. I've just been really busy with work and...stuff."

"Good to know," Colin said with a half-smile. "So would one of the things you've been busy with be museum guy?"

Savannah immediately felt awkward but reminded herself that Colin was just a friend. "Yeah, a little. We had our third date last night."

"Wow, that's a big one," he said with a wink.

"Is it?"

Colin's response was to wiggle his eyebrows, and suddenly Savannah got his drift. "NO! It wasn't that kind of date. We just went to dinner and then he took me to this storytelling show over at the 9:30 Club." Savannah could feel her face growing bright red and looked away from him while taking another sip of her coffee.

"Wow, museums and storytelling at the 9:30 Club? This guy's going all out on the unique dates thing. That's cool. I mean, he's probably not trying to compensate for any...shortcomings," Colin teased.

"You're such a...guy!" Savannah said, throwing a napkin at him while trying not to laugh.

Colin had hit a little close to what Savannah had been worrying about since the previous night. She and Steve had sat close together during the show and leaned against each other as they laughed, and he'd touched her knee a few times. They'd even had a little make-out session tucked into a dark corner near the door as they waited for the Uber he'd ordered for her, and it had been really...nice. But that was all. Still, nice was good. It was definitely better than...not nice, right?

"He's a gentleman," she said as she dodged a return hit from the napkin. "Maybe you've heard of it? We're just taking it slow."

"If you say so, Red."

Hearing him use her nickname felt so comforting that Savannah almost said something about it. Instead, she flung the napkin ball back at him.

They were still grinning at each other like idiots when Crystal came out onto the patio.

"Colin? Can I see you for a second?"

Savannah glanced up, surprised by how stressed Crystal sounded. She was normally so cheerful and energetic. Savannah now saw dark circles under her eyes, and she almost seemed jittery.

Colin stood and followed Crystal around the corner of the building, out of earshot, but Savannah could still see them. She told herself it was none of her business, but she couldn't help watching them and trying to figure out what they were talking about. They both seemed agitated.

At one point, Crystal raised her voice and said, "You can't just refuse all of a sudden." And later, "I'll pay you whatever you want!"

Then Savannah thought she heard Colin say, "It's not about the money," and something about trouble with his supplier.

Eventually they seemed to come to an agreement, and Savannah heard Colin say "last time."

Crystal went back inside looking relieved and miserable at the same time, and Savannah had a cold feeling in the pit of her stomach. There had to be an innocent explanation for what she'd just seen, but she was having trouble coming up with it.

Colin came over to her table but didn't sit down. "I've gotta go take care of some stuff, but it was good to see you, Red."

"Everything OK?" Savannah asked, standing up so she could be eye level with him.

"Yeah, it's just...business." He started to walk away, hands stuffed in his pockets, then turned back and said, "You should bring this guy by the bar sometime. Let me make sure he's good enough for you."

She smiled and said, "Maybe I will."

Colin nodded then walked quickly away.

Savannah sat back down and picked at her scone. She thought back over some of the other interactions she'd observed between Crystal and Colin and realized that whatever was going on, it had been going on for a while.

Chapter 16

A few days later, Colin was still brooding over his
conversation with Crystal, but he perked up when he
saw a text from Savannah on his phone after he got off work—
until he read it.

*I was thinking of bringing Steve by for brunch on Saturday morning so
you can meet him. Does that work?*

Colin pictured Savannah and this guy strolling in to brunch
like most couples did—announcing to the world that they'd just
rolled out of bed together. He felt bile rise at the back of his
throat, but then he reminded himself that he had known this
was a possibility when he'd set his plan in motion. He needed
to see it through. And if this guy fit her Plan, then the sooner
Colin knew he'd failed, the sooner he could move on.

So he typed, *Yep. I'll reserve your table for you. 11am.*

Saturday morning a few minutes before 11, Savannah walked
into a lively and crowded Zipped. She was surprised to see the
space transformed into the spitting image of her vision of the
afterlife. A U-shaped buffet to the right of the door took up
the end of the bar, the stage area, and one bay window. It was
piled high with all manner of pastries and fruit and held large
dispensers of mimosas and Bloody Marys. At the other end of
the room, in front of the booths, was an elaborate omelet and
waffle station.

Savannah was relieved to see a RESERVED sign on her
usual table because there wasn't another open seat in the place.
Sliding into her chair, she glanced around for Colin and saw
him moving between tables, chatting, refilling coffee mugs,
and clearing plates with the grace of an athlete on the field.
The white towel hanging out of the back pocket of his jeans

drew her eye to the way the muscles in his thighs and tight butt moved.

A few minutes after 11, he suddenly looked over at Savannah's table, as though he had just now remembered that she would be there. He nodded at her while he finished processing a check, and then he made his way over to her table carrying a silver carafe.

"Morning, Red," Colin said as he poured her a cup of coffee. "Where's your friend?"

"He's running a few minutes late, but he'll be here."

"You guys didn't come over together?" he said before he could stop himself.

Savannah narrowed her eyes at him. "I know what you're asking, and not that it's any of your business, but no, we didn't see each other last night. He's supposed to meet me here."

"Hey, I was just making conversation," Colin said, unable to hide his smile.

At 11:30, he came over to refill her coffee cup. "Why don't you go get an omelet or a waffle? If someone comes in looking like he's lost, I'll direct him to your table."

Savannah sighed. "Might as well."

"Have you called him?"

"Yeah, he's at work. First he said he'd be ten minutes late, then another ten minutes, and now he's saying he's not sure."

"Well, he's an idiot for putting work before you," Colin said then quickly turned and went back to the bar.

When Savannah got back to her table with her tomato-and-cheese omelet, she found a mimosa and chocolate donut waiting for her. She looked over and saw Colin watching her from the bar. She mouthed the word "thanks," and he responded with the smile and wink that she was getting very used to seeing.

At 1:00, the brunch was officially over and only a handful of people lingered over their coffee.

"So you got stood up, huh?" Colin said, dropping into the chair across from her.

"Looks like," Savannah said glumly. "Around noon he texted to say that he would text me when he was on his way, and I haven't heard from him since." She gestured toward her phone like it was at fault.

"The guy's a loser, but you shouldn't let it get you down. Better to know now."

"I know. I'm probably just having a sugar crash." She looked down at the remnants of what had been a second donut and a chocolate croissant that she'd used to distract herself for the past hour.

As much as Colin had hated the idea of her being at brunch with another guy, he hated even more that she was so down because it hadn't worked out.

"Hey, you wanna get out of here?" he asked suddenly.

Savannah had her head propped on her hand and was drawing designs in the pastry crumbs on the table. "What do you mean?" she asked without looking up.

"I mean let's go do something. It's a gorgeous day, I've been working around the clock for weeks, and you're not doing much better."

"What do you want to do?" she asked, finally looking at him.

"I don't know, but we'll figure something out. Give me five minutes and I'll meet you out front." Colin stood and took a step away from the table before turning back. "You're in, right?"

"I'm in," Savannah answered with a grin that lit up her green eyes and made Colin feel like the luckiest guy in the world to be the recipient of it.

As Savannah gathered her stuff and headed outside into a beautiful, warm sunny day, Colin ducked into the kitchen to let everyone know he was taking off.

Diana looked shocked. "Really?" she asked.

"Is there a problem?" Colin said as he washed his hands and splashed water on his face.

"No, but you never take time off. What's the occasion?"

"I just realized how long it's been since I saw daylight. Or had fun." He pulled off his dirty T-shirt and changed into the clean one he kept on a hook on the back of his office door. Having seen him do this multiple times, Diana didn't bat an eye at his six-pack abs.

"So no catfish nuggets today?" she said.

"She got stood up so I'm going to try to cheer her up." He looked at his reflection in the small mirror on his office wall and ran a hand through his hair.

"I can't believe I've known you for five years and I'm only just now realizing how much of a masochist you are," Diana said as she watched him primp.

Colin shot her an annoyed look. "I'm not a masochist. I'm just…" the words "crazy about her" popped into his head, but he wasn't ready to let that out into the world, so instead he said, "I'm just going to have some fun."

Diana followed him out into the restaurant. "Well, if this doesn't end up being torturous enough, I know some special clubs that might interest you."

"You're hilarious, D."

"You know, the kind that are in basements, without names."

"Goodbye, Diana," Colin called over his shoulder as he pulled open the door.

"I've got an idea," he said as he joined Savannah on the sidewalk.

"Good, because I have no ideas."

"Do you like baseball?" Colin asked as they started walking south toward the waterfront.

"Why? Are we going to a game?" Savannah asked, the excitement evident in her voice.

Laughing, Colin said, "I guess we'd better be, with that reaction."

"I've never been to a game, but it's on my D.C.-specific bucket list."

"Do you do anything without a plan or a list, Red?"

"Not often," she admitted.

"Well, then brace yourself, honey, because today is going to be very unplanned."

Savannah felt a tingle race through her body, but she wasn't sure if it was nerves, excitement, or the fact that as they walked, his arm kept brushing against hers.

When they arrived at Nationals Park half an hour later, the game was already underway, though there were still a lot of people milling around outside having a few drinks before going into the stadium.

"It's OK," Colin reassured her. "Nothing interesting happens during the first inning anyway."

After she and Colin passed through the metal detectors at the outer edge of the stadium, Savannah headed toward the ticket sales booth, which had a long line of people waiting, but Colin put his hand on her lower back and steered her away.

"Let's not waste time in that line. I've got a better idea." He quickly walked away from the crowds and toward the delivery entry into the ballpark.

"What are we doing?" Savannah asked. "I thought we were going to the game."

"We are," he said with a smile. "We're just going to use the back way."

"The back way? Wait—are we sneaking in?" Savannah was shocked but also feeling that tingle again.

"Eh, sneaking sounds devious. Let's think of it as using an alternate entry point."

As they rounded a corner, Colin thought he recognized the security guard idly pacing near the delivery entrance, thumbs hooked on his gun belt.

"Hang here for a second," he said. "I'll be right back."

Colin hurried over to the guard, who smiled and bumped fists with him in greeting. It looked like they were joking around a little, then Colin motioned toward her, held his hands palms up, and shrugged his shoulders, and he and the security guard laughed. Then Colin reached into his pocket and shifted his body so that his back was to her. The other man took whatever Colin handed him and slapped Colin on the shoulder. They exchanged a few more words and another a fist bump, and Colin trotted back to Savannah.

"Ready to go in?" he asked.

"What was all that?"

"That's Tyrell. I know him from...ah...my basketball league." Colin had his hand on her back and was propelling her toward the door. As they approached, Tyrell swiped his security pass and opened the door for them.

"You kids have fun in there," he said with a smile as they passed through.

"I didn't know you played basketball," Savannah said.

"There's a lot you don't know about me, Red." The truth of that statement didn't sit right with her, but he said it in a low voice with his mouth close to her ear, giving her goose bumps over her whole body. "Now let's hurry before someone sees us."

"This is crazy!" Savannah whispered. Her cheeks were flushed, and her eyes were sparkling with excitement.

Since she seemed to be enjoying the cloak-and-dagger stuff so much, Colin decided to keep it up, even though it wasn't strictly necessary that they sneak around.

They reached the end of the hall, and he held a finger to his lips to signal her to be quiet. Then he slowly poked his head around the corner and, seeing that the next hallway was also empty, pulled her after him, and they ran down the hall toward a closed door.

Colin pushed open the door, which led into a stairwell. As Savannah moved toward it, a door slammed loudly somewhere nearby. Colin pulled Savannah to him with a little more force than he'd intended, causing her to fall against his chest. He wrapped his arm around her to keep her there and took a step back into the stairwell so the door closed behind them. He looked down into her upturned face, felt the warmth of her hands on his chest, and was suddenly aware only of the sound of their breathing.

Savannah's head was filled with the sound of her pounding heart. Colin's chest was firm and warm under her hands, and she wanted so badly to slide her fingers up his neck to his hair and see if it was as soft as it looked.

His eyes traveled from her emerald eyes down to her full lips, which were slightly parted as her breath escaped in little pants. And he knew she wanted him just as much as he wanted her.

He slowly inched his face closer to hers. When their lips were millimeters apart, Savannah's eyes drifted closed.

And then a door slammed right above them, and they both jumped. At the sound of feet running down the flights of stairs, Savannah jumped back from Colin and stared at him with panic in her eyes. Colin grabbed her hand and pulled her back into a dark corner behind the stairs, where he flatted himself against the wall and held her tightly against his chest. Seconds later, a man came barreling down the stairs, threw the door open, and rushed out, not even noticing Savannah and Colin in their inadequate hiding place.

As soon as the man was gone, Savannah looked up at Colin and said, "That was close."

Colin debated saying they were still in danger of being caught so he could keep her pressed up against him for a little while longer but decided not to overplay his hand. "Yeah, let's hurry before someone else comes through."

As Savannah followed Colin up the stairs, she tried to calm the butterflies that had taken flight in her stomach the moment he had pulled her against him. She wasn't a casual making-out-in-stairwells kind of girl, but she suspected that if Colin had kissed her, she would have become one immediately because one kiss would not have been nearly enough.

Three flights up, Colin stopped at a door and looked through its small window to survey the concourse. It was crowded with people getting food, heading to the restrooms, or standing around watching the game through the entrances to the stands. He opened the door a crack and looked out to confirm that the coast was clear, then he closed the door and turned to Savannah.

"Here's the plan," he said. "I'm going to open the door, and you're going to slip through and blend into the crowd as quickly as possible while moving down the concourse to the left. Walk to the first restroom and then hang out there, and I'll catch up in a minute. OK?"

Savannah's eyes were bright, and her skin still held a flush from earlier, making her look completely delectable. Taking a deep breath and squaring her shoulders, she said, "Got it."

"You can do this, Red," he said. And he reached out to tuck her hair behind her ear.

Savannah's eyes went wide, but otherwise she didn't acknowledge the intimacy of the gesture. Instead, she nodded her readiness. Colin took one more look through the window before pulling the door open and pushing Savannah out. He watched as she held her head up and calmly but quickly moved into the flow of the crowd. After a moment, he slipped out and hurried to catch up with her.

When Savannah reached the restrooms, she paced around waiting for Colin and gave herself a pep talk about sticking to The Plan. This was definitely an exciting day, and sure, she was attracted to him—she was only human, right? But just because she had those feelings did not mean she had to act on them. Acting on them would be very detrimental to The Plan.

Or would it? She was starting to wonder if Rayne was right. Maybe it was possible to give in to her attraction to Colin without jeopardizing her overall goal.

As she was turning around to pace in the other direction, she caught sight of Colin less than twenty feet away talking to a tall, slim, beautiful woman who managed to look elegant even in jeans and a simple linen blouse. She was smiling at him as she talked, and when she reached out to touch his arm, Savannah saw the glitter of what looked like a very expensive gold watch. Colin was smiling back at her and didn't seem to be in any hurry to end the conversation and find Savannah. Then the woman's expression became more serious, and she leaned a little closer to Colin.

Without thinking it through, Savannah charged toward them. As she reached Colin's side, the woman was saying something about missing inventory and he replied with, "Don't worry about it. I'll take care of it."

"Colin! There you are," Savannah said.

The woman turned to look at her. Up close, she was older than Savannah had thought, around forty, but she looked good. Her short blond hair was cut in a fashionable wispy style, and her makeup was flawless. Savannah was suddenly deeply embarrassed, and her stomach was in knots. So this was what jealousy felt like.

But she reminded herself that she had no claim on Colin and was desperately trying to come up with a graceful way out of there, out of the whole damn stadium, when he said, "Savannah! Honey! There you are!" He put his arm around her and pulled her close. "I'm sorry to have kept you waiting."

Savannah stared at him, surprised at his seeming eagerness to call in an order of catfish nuggets with this elegant woman, but then after weeks of improvising scenes like this, she jumped right in.

"You know any amount of time without you is too long," she said as she ran a finger along his jawline and noticed, in spite of herself, the pleasant way his slight stubble tickled.

Colin leaned in like he was nuzzling her neck and whispered "Save me" against her ear. His hot breath on her sensitive ear made fireworks light off from her belly and flood her veins with heat, and she jerked away before things got hot for real.

Forcing a giggle, she swatted his chest. "Oh, you!"

Colin grinned and turned to the woman. "Excuse my rudeness, Holly. This is Savannah. Savannah, this is Holly. She's... uh...an old family friend."

"I'm not as old as all that," Holly said good-naturedly. "Pleased to meet you, Savannah." She held out her hand, and Savannah took it, noticing her professional manicure and wondering—if this woman truly was a family friend—just what sort of circles Colin's family moved in.

"I'm glad I ran into you today, Colin," Holly said. "Let me know when you've taken care of that business we talked about. I need to get everything straightened out as soon as possible."

"Sure, of course," Colin said, his arm still tight around Savannah. She felt a tremor of impatience—or maybe it was nervousness?—go through him.

"You know how the boss is about things like this," Holly said with a smile. She nodded at Savannah and then walked off toward the concession stands, and Colin steered Savannah in the opposite direction, his arm around her shoulder.

"I owe you one, Red."

"Yeah, you looked like you were really suffering," she said as she pushed Colin's arm away.

He thought about explaining that Holly was also a business associate, but that might lead into dangerous territory. Besides, he kind of liked the jealous vibe Savannah was giving off.

"An old 'friend,' huh?" she said. "As in someone you used to sleep with?" She hoped her tone sounded light, not hurt or jealous—even though she wanted to go back and claw that woman's eyes out with an intensity she'd never experienced before.

"I didn't say that. But why do you care anyway? Are you jealous?" Colin smiled and tugged a strand of her hair as they walked.

"No!" Savannah said, swatting his hand away. "It's none of my business who you sleep with."

"If you say so. Although I think I'm gonna start calling you Green instead of Red."

"You're delusional."

He stopped walking and turned to face her. "Seriously, Red, there is nothing and never was anything between Holly and me. Except business." Then he quickly added, "And family, of course."

She thought back to the conversation she'd burst in on. "Is everything OK at Zipped? What was that business Holly was talking about?"

Colin glanced away for a moment then said, "She's in charge of inventory. There was a mix-up, and I told her I'd straighten it out. It's not a big deal." Colin mentally crossed his fingers that Savannah wouldn't ask any more questions.

The answer sounded plausible, but Savannah wasn't entirely at ease even when he finally looked her in the eye.

"So she's not a family friend?" she asked, wondering why he'd bother to lie.

"She is. But she's also a business associate."

Savannah must have looked as confused as she felt because he suddenly grabbed her hand and said, "Come on. We came here to forget about work and rotten dates—let's have some fun."

She laughed as he nearly dragged her around the last bend of the concourse and into an open food court area, with huge TVs showing the game and a long counter that overlooked the field where people could eat and drink.

"How 'bout you go find us a spot at the counter while I grab us some beers?" he asked.

By the time Colin returned with two beers, two hot dogs, and a bucket of french fries, Savannah had secured a tight spot in the center of the counter with a perfect view of the field.

"I was also going to get you some cotton candy, but figured I'd save some leverage for later," he said.

Savannah picked up her hot dog but immediately put it down. There was an icky hard lump in the pit of her stomach—the same icky hard lump that had started to form when she pictured Colin with other women, with any other woman, and she didn't like what it meant about her feelings.

"Something wrong?" Colin asked around a bite of hot dog.

"Still full from brunch, I guess."

"Right! Sorry. I'll eat your dog," he said as he crammed the last bite of his own hot dog into his mouth.

Over the next hour, Savannah drank her beer and nibbled on french fries and got absorbed in the game. The counter was prime real estate, and eventually Colin moved to stand behind her, his arms braced on the counter to keep her from being jostled by the drunk and rowdy people on either side of her. His body was warm against hers, and she couldn't believe how comfortable it felt to have him hovering behind her, leaning in to offer commentary on the game or the people around them.

It didn't take long before that knot in her stomach was replaced with a warm glow, and the only thoughts in her head were of this moment, with Colin, hoping she could hide from the real world with him forever. A little voice in the back of her head told her she was in a danger zone, but she pushed those thoughts into a box labeled "worries for later" and kept her mind in the moment. This deliciously warm and exciting moment of being so close to Colin.

During the game, they heard an announcement that there would be a concert afterward. "Oh, I've always wanted to go to one of those concerts!" Savannah said, turning slightly within the frame of Colin's arms. "I've seen them on TV, and they look so fun, all the people down on the field dancing."

"Then we'll stay for the concert." Colin watched the smile spread across Savannah's face and knew, without a doubt, that he'd do anything in his power to make her smile like that as often as possible.

Chapter 17

By the sixth inning, Savannah was tired of fighting for space at the counter so she and Colin walked along the concourse, people-watching and idly chatting between companionable silences. At some point, her hand slipped inside his, and she chose to leave it there. As the game ended and the announcer told them they had an hour before the concert started, Savannah asked, "Won't we need tickets to get into the show?"

"I bet if we stayed up here we'd be fine, but getting onto the field might be a little tricky."

"Ah, well, that's OK, I'm sure we can dance just as well up here as on the field," she said, meaning it. The day had felt like one of the best dates she'd ever been on, and she decided to stop reminding herself that it wasn't and let herself pretend, just for the day.

"I might have a few tricks up my sleeve yet," Colin said with a wink.

Savannah laughed. "Just don't get us arrested, OK?" She bumped her shoulder against his, and Colin casually draped an arm around her shoulder. And she didn't pull away.

"I make no promises, Red," he said and had to stop himself from kissing the top of her head.

They went into the stadium and walked up the ramp to the highest level of seats, to the very top row, where he dropped into a seat and pulled her down next to him.

"No one is going to give a damn if we have tickets for these seats or not," he said, propping his feet on the back of the seat in front of him.

"My god, the view from up here is amazing." Savannah leaned forward and craned her neck to look down across the field to the city skyline.

"It definitely is."

Savannah turned and found Colin staring at her. A small laugh, almost more of a snort, escaped from her lips. Colin looked at her in surprise and then started to laugh, too.

"You're so cheesy," she said, full-out laughing now.

"I know. I know!" Colin tilted his head back and covered his face with his hands. "In my head, it sounded like a line from a movie, but when I said it…"

Savannah screamed with laughter. "It *is* a line from a movie, dork. That's *why* it's cheesy."

"Fine, laugh! I deserve it," Colin said, laughing, too. But when he turned to look at Savannah, the laugh died in his throat. The setting sun glinted off her chestnut hair and her green eyes sparkled, and he didn't think he'd ever seen anyone so beautiful in his life.

"Savannah—" he said in a voice rough with desire.

She turned to look at him, and suddenly she wasn't laughing anymore either. The tension between them was so thick Savannah knew what was going to happen next if she didn't do something.

Colin slid sideways in his chair until his knees touched hers. Reaching up to brush her hair from her face, he saw her gaze drift down to his mouth and he couldn't breathe. Then her eyes darted up to meet his, and she exhaled what sounded like "yes."

He ran his fingers through her hair to rest lightly at the base of her skull, and her hands moved to his chest. He leaned his mouth a millimeter closer, and she grabbed a handful of his T-shirt and pressed her lips against his.

When Colin had stopped laughing and looked at her with so much intensity, she knew he was going to kiss her. She knew, deep in her heart that they'd been leading to this all day. A small warning bell started to sound, but she promptly shut it down. Just for today, she was going to be *this* girl. The girl without a plan, the one who gets to kiss the insanely hot guy at the baseball stadium and not have it mean anything.

When their lips touched, Savannah felt like it was the first and only kiss she'd ever had. The whole world dropped away, and the only sensations she cared about were the warmth of his lips against hers and his spicy-sweet scent. After only a few seconds—not nearly long enough—Colin pulled back, and Savannah opened her eyes to see a question in his. She let go of the fistful of his shirt she'd been clutching and slid her hands up the side of his neck until her palms were on his jaw and slowly pulled his mouth back to hers, which was all the confirmation he needed.

His tongue slid between her lips and glided over hers like silk. He tasted faintly of beer and something else, something fresh and masculine and strangely familiar. As he tangled his hands in her hair and shifted to deepen the kiss, Savannah heard a low moan and realized it had come from her. Colin responded by catching her bottom lip between his teeth and giving a gentle tug. Then he leaned his forehead against hers while they both caught their breath.

"Holy crap," Savannah breathed.

"Holy crap indeed."

She could hear the smile in his voice and couldn't resist pressing her lips against his again. He responded immediately, filling her mouth with his hot, probing tongue, one hand firmly at the back of her head and one hand moving up and down her back.

With a rough, masculine growl, he ripped himself away and flopped back in his seat, panting for air. Savannah still sat on the edge of her seat, turned toward him, knees touching. She brought her fingers up to touch her swollen lips and looked out over the field. Colin's hand slid from her shoulders down her back and tugged her toward him. She let him pull her in until her head rested on his shoulder, and then he kissed the top of her head, something he'd wanted to do all day.

Blowing out another lungful of air, he said, "Good lord, woman." His voice was still rough with desire, and the sound made Savannah lift her head up and try to get him to kiss her again. "You stop that, or I'm going to do things to you that will get us both arrested."

Just then his phone chimed in his pocket. "Saved by the bell," he murmured.

He pulled the phone out and looked at the message on the screen before shoving it back in his pocket. Her head was resting on his shoulder and her face was turned up to his, her mouth looking eminently kissable. He let out another breath and stood up, pulling her with him.

"How about we go check out this concert that's about to start?" he said.

"We can see it just fine from here." Savannah wrapped her arms around his neck. Now that she'd given in to her attraction, she felt like she would never have her fill. But she was also afraid to do anything to break the spell, scared they'd never get back to this place. And Savannah really, really liked this place.

"Red, you know as well as I do that if we stay up here, we're not watching this concert, and the things I'll end up doing to you deserve a better setting than dirty stadium seats."

He wrapped his arms around her waist and pulled her tightly against him, letting her feel exactly how serious he was about his intentions. She opened her mouth to protest, but he cut her off. "Nope. Now go, and I'll be right behind you. I just need a minute before I can navigate the steps comfortably." Colin smiled ruefully as he adjusted his now very snug jeans.

Savannah took a step toward the aisle then turned back to look at him, fearing that this would all evaporate. Seeming to read her mind, Colin closed the gap between them and took her by the shoulders. "I'll be right behind you. Our day isn't nearly over. There's still much fun to be had, OK?"

Nodding, Savannah smiled and said, "OK."

"OK." Colin dropped a light kiss on her forehead and turned her toward the aisle with a pat on the butt.

When Savannah got to the bottom and started down the ramp, she glanced up and saw Colin typing on his phone. The thought that he'd been trying to get rid of her for reasons other than modesty crossed her mind, but she shoved it into the "worries for later" box, not wanting to ruin the spell of the day.

Colin caught up to her on the concourse a few minutes later, and she suddenly felt shy. Having had a moment to catch her breath and clear her head, she kept thinking, "Did I just have the hottest make-out session of my life with *Colin*?" She had an urge to text Rayne but didn't because Rayne was real world, this was still pretend land, and in pretend land, Savannah did whatever she wanted with sexy, funny, not-part-of-The-Plan Colin.

"Ready?" he asked with a smile as he took her hand and led her to the elevators. Savannah glanced down at their entwined fingers, liking what she saw.

As they stood side by side in the elevator, neither of them spoke, but they kept glancing at each other and giggling like teenagers. As soon as the doors opened, they could hear the band starting to play, and there were swarms of people everywhere. Colin motioned for Savannah to walk out ahead of him and she did, only to walk straight into a security guard. Quickly backing up, she found herself pressed against Colin's chest. He put his mouth by her ear and said, "We're fine. Just act natural and follow me."

Savannah couldn't suppress the thrill that ran down her spine as Colin whispered into her ear. He made a mental note that that was definitely a sweet spot for her.

Stepping in front of her and reaching back for her hand, Colin steered them around the bored-looking security guard and straight for the gateway to the field and a sign that said "VIP Access Only."

Savannah was wondering if he was going to jump the fence and make her run for it, but then he pulled a laminated card out of his pocket and flashed it at the guard, who nodded and opened the gate. Savannah's mouth fell open as he tugged her out onto the field.

"How?" she said gesturing toward the gate, not even sure what to ask first.

Looping his arms around her waist, he said, "Come on, Red, did you think I'd let you down? You said you wanted to be on the field, and you're on the field."

Running her hands around his waist and then snaking one hand into his back pocket, she had the pass in her hand before he realized she wasn't just copping a feel. He let go of her and tried to grab the pass from her, but she jumped out of his reach and read, "STAFF. ALL ACCESS."

She looked up at him with narrowed eyes. "Where did you get this?"

He could see the wheels turning in her head as she no doubt thought back to the security guard and Holly and the text he'd just gotten. God, he didn't want to blow this now, not when she was finally looking at him—and kissing him—the way he'd dreamed about.

"I have a friend who works here, and he owed me a favor so I texted him earlier, and then I met up with him right before I met back up with you," he said, rushing to get the words out before she could change her mind about him.

Savannah considered his story for a second before deciding it was plausible—or plausible enough for pretend land and this easygoing version of Savannah. Handing the pass back to him, she said, "You're just full of surprises, aren't you?"

Flooded with relief, he pulled her in for a quick kiss and then said, "Let's go do some dancing!"

The band was an alternative country band with a rocky, folky sound that was perfect for dancing. Watching Colin move next to her with seemingly no inhibitions made Savannah start to seriously wonder if this was all an elaborate dream. She said a fervent prayer that if it was, she wouldn't wake up anytime soon.

When the band transitioned into a slow song, Colin pulled Savannah to him, one hand loose around her waist, the other holding her hand pressed against his chest. Savannah rested her head against his cheek. He leaned close to her ear and whispered, "I'm not sure how much longer I can stand you wiggling against me like this."

His breath sent an electrical current through her body, and she burrowed her face into his neck to catch her breath. He put both arms around her waist, pressed her closer against him, and said, "Are you trying to drive me insane?"

She smiled up at him and kissed him. After a minute, his hands slid down to rest lightly on her backside. When her only reaction was to deepen the kiss, Colin tightened his grip and then dropped his mouth to her neck just below her ear.

"Yup, you are definitely trying to make me lose my mind," he said. "Or at least get me arrested."

Savannah laughed, overwhelmed by how good all this felt. She'd never had a man be so obviously hot for her, and she'd never felt this attractive and comfortable and free in her life.

The song ended and was followed by a faster song, and Colin pushed her back a little. Savannah looked at him in surprise. He kissed the tip of her nose and said, "I just need a little space before I embarrass myself like an over-eager sixteen-year-old."

"Oh!" Savannah said as she realized what he was saying. "Oh, OK." She dropped her arms from around his neck and turned to stand next to him as they faced the stage.

"No, now you're too far away." He reached over and pulled her in front of him. "Much better." He pulled her tight against him and wrapped his arms around her waist. Feeling uncharacteristically daring, she pressed her backside against his crotch and wiggled slightly.

"Is this better?" she teased.

"Not really," Colin said, sounding like he was in pain. Savannah started to move away, but he held her tight. "Worth it," he said with a little nip at her earlobe.

For the next few minutes, they stood together like that, and Savannah enjoyed the unfamiliar feeling of complete contentment with an undercurrent of electricity, wondering where this night was going to end up, but in no hurry for it to end.

"Damn, you have got such a sweet ass," Colin said with a visceral growl in her ear that was possibly the sexiest sound Savannah had ever heard. Turning to face him, she pulled his mouth to hers and sucked in his tongue as if she intended to swallow him whole.

When they finally broke the kiss to catch their breath, Colin's hands were firmly planted on her backside and the collar of his

T-shirt was twisted in her fists.

"You wanna get out of here?" he asked, his voice scratchy with desire.

"Yes, please," Savannah said even as she continued to press her body harder against his.

"Red, you are literally killing me right now." Colin dropped a quick hard kiss on her swollen lips and then reached up to take her hands from his collar and lead them off the field as fast as he could get through the crowd. Once they were clear, he practically broke into a run toward the stadium exit signs.

Laughing, Savannah ran to keep up with him. Never had she had a man act like this around her, and she was loving it.

They burst through the exit turnstiles and out onto the sidewalk, where a line of cabs stood waiting for fares. Colin stopped suddenly and turned toward Savannah with a questioning look. "Your place?" she asked, eyes focused on his mouth, wondering if she could even wait that long to kiss him again.

"Thank god," Colin said and headed for the first taxi in line. "Get in," he growled in that way that made her legs go weak.

Without another word, she crawled into the cab and across the seat. Colin slid in beside her and, after nearly shouting the address at the driver, turned to look at Savannah.

Taking in her flushed face and chest, her heavy breathing and eyes dark with desire, he leaned toward her, and in the next second, their lips were together and his hand was tangled in her hair. As his hand slid down to her waist, grazing the side of her chest, Savannah's breath caught and Colin cursed the fact that they were still in public.

"We're here!" the driver announced, startling Savannah, who had completely forgotten they weren't alone.

Colin dug some bills out of his pocket and tossed them onto the front seat before grabbing Savannah's hand and pulling her out of the cab. They pushed through a low wrought-iron gate and practically ran up the sidewalk to the front door of a large brick townhouse. On the porch, Colin grabbed Savannah and pushed her up against a column, greedily capturing her mouth in his as his hands moved up her body to cup her breasts.

"Oh my god, Savannah," he murmured as he felt her nipples harden through the thin cotton of her bra and T-shirt. "You're so soft, so hot."

"Door," Savannah gasped. "Inside," she squeaked, not sure how much longer her legs were going to hold her.

Pulling her against him and continuing to kiss her, he turned her with him as he punched a code into a panel by the door, only letting her go as he pulled the door open and gestured for her to walk through in front of him. He pulled the door closed behind them, wrapped his arm around her waist, and steered her past a wooden staircase to a door at the end of the hallway.

As he struggled to dig his keys out of his pocket, he whispered, "Please don't be here, Chase, please don't be here," and then pushed open the door.

It was dark and silent inside, but just to be sure, Colin called out, "Chase? You home?"

When there was no response, he turned to Savannah with a grin and nudged her back against the closed door. Then he took her hands and raised them above her head and held them there while he brushed his lips against her ear and said, "Where were we?"

Savannah squirmed against the door in a delicious agony she'd never experienced before while he dropped butterfly kisses along the sensitive skin between her ear and shoulder. Turning her head, she tried to catch his mouth with her own, but he remained just out of reach and teased her by flicking his tongue over her skin.

Savannah's knees started to buckle. She had been with a few other men—a boyfriend in high school and a couple in college—but sex had never been like this. It had always been fine. Nice even, if she was lucky. There had been some amount of desire, but never anything like this. This was carnal and visceral. Want and need and something primal all at once.

"Oh god, Colin. Please. Touch me. Let me touch you," Savannah panted, surprised at her own boldness and yet not at all embarrassed.

"Anything," Colin said releasing her.

She ran her hands over the flat muscles of his stomach and over the tight, well-formed ass, and finally around to the front. She brushed her hands lightly along his zipper, causing him to catch his breath and thrilling Savannah with her ability to affect him.

She moved her hands up under his shirt until he raised his arms and let her pull the shirt off. She ran her hands lightly down his chest, taking a moment to admire his well-defined muscles. Colin held himself still, letting her set the pace, relishing her attention. She lightly traced the outline of the compass tattoo on his biceps.

"I've only seen the little part that poked out of your shirts," she whispered. "I've been desperate to see all of it." Then she turned her attention to a complicated interwoven design on his left pec and said, "I knew there would be more. This is beautiful."

She traced her fingers over the tattoo, her breath hot on his chest, challenging his self-control. When she leaned forward and touched her lips to the tattoo and flicked his nipple with her tongue, he moaned and gave up.

He slid his hands under her shirt and tugged at her bra, causing her own sharp intake of breath as she arched her back and thrust herself more firmly into his hands. Without taking his mouth or hands off her body, Colin maneuvered them toward his room and through the open door. As he kicked the door shut behind them, Savannah slipped her hands inside the waistband of his jeans and pulled him toward the bed.

He tugged her shirt over her head, and she quickly undid the button of his jeans, slid his zipper down, and pressed her hands against the hard, hot ridge that was separated from her touch by only a thin pair of boxers. Colin gasped as he pressed himself against her.

"You need to go easy, Red, or this will be over before you know it."

He pushed her back until she fell flat on the bed. Expecting him to fall on top of her, Savannah held her arms out, but Colin kept his feet on the floor, planted a hand on either side of her head, and began trailing warm wet kisses down her neck and shoulders. With one hand, he yanked her bra strap and then her entire bra down as he progressed.

"Please," Savannah moaned, arching her back.

Moving down to her belly, leaving a feather trail of kisses and hot breath, he undid the zipper on her shorts and yanked them off in one fluid motion.

"My god, Savannah. You are so beautiful," Colin breathed as he looked down at her lying on his bed in nothing but her panties—a moment he'd fantasized about more than he wanted to admit.

He leaned down and kissed her with an intensity that he briefly worried would overwhelm her until he realized she was matching his intensity. Savannah's hands scraped up and down his back. Then she tugged at the waistband of his jeans and murmured, "Off."

Colin stripped off his jeans and boxers. Savannah propped herself up on her elbows and said, "You're...amazing. So beautiful."

With a growl of desire, Colin launched himself at Savannah, wanting to touch and taste every inch of her. As her warm hands press against his crotch, he moaned. "I'm serious, honey, if you keep doing that, this is going to be over before it starts."

"That's OK," Savannah said as she flicked her tongue across one of his nipples and elicited a sharp hiss from him. Pushing him over onto his back, she eagerly began to explore.

"I want to make this last," he said. "I want to explore every part of you, I want...oh god."

Savannah smiled as he lost his train of thought. She dropped kisses across his abdomen, and as she moved back up his body, she let her hair trail over his chest, loving how labored his breathing had become. She'd never imagined it would be such a turn-on to know that she could turn him on this much.

She wanted to keep exploring his body and the kinds of reactions she could elicit, but he planted his hands firmly on her ass and pulled her so the length of her body was covering his.

"Do you have a condom?" she whispered against his ear.

"A who? Oh! A...yeah, yes," Colin said.

He made that low growl again that was fast becoming Savannah's favorite sound, and grasping her by the hips, quickly flipped her onto her back. Propped up on his elbow, he took a moment to look her over from head to toe. Feeling suddenly shy, Savannah moved to cover herself, but he stopped her.

"Let me look at you," he whispered. "You're stunning." He traced her lips with his fingers and then let them trail down her body before leaning down to take one of her nipples in his mouth.

Arching her back and tangling her hands in his hair, she called out his name and he growled again.

"This is going to be amazing," he whispered with a smile and pressed his lips hard against hers before moving farther up the bed to reach into his night stand. A few seconds later, he was back beside her, propped up on his elbow and looking down at her. She pulled his head down for a kiss.

"Are you sure about this?" he asked.

"I don't know that I've ever wanted anything, or anyone, more," she said, lifting her head to kiss him again.

"I know things moved pretty fast today," he said in between kisses. "I don't want to mess with your Plan—"

"Colin, please. I'm sure. So, so, SO sure."

Moving his hands in teasing circles on her stomach and thighs, Colin bent down to her ear. "Pinky swear?"

She made a series of incoherent sounds as she arched her back and writhed against him. Slowly his fingers moved where she wanted them, to her very center, and she nearly cried out with relief.

"God, sweetheart, you're so wet," Colin murmured, moving his fingers against her. In response, Savannah grabbed the condom that he'd set by her hip and pushed it at him.

"This. Now. On. Now." She couldn't form a coherent sentence, but she didn't care.

He took the condom from the wrapper and quickly rolled it on. Then he hovered above her, his knees between her legs.

He paused. Her eyes closed and her lips parted slightly, waiting. After a second, she opened her eyes to find his eyes almost black with desire staring down at her. Without breaking eye contact, he slowly slid inside her.

"Oh, Christ," Colin said, dropping down to bury his face in her neck.

"OH god. Oh YES," Savannah cried out, scraping her nails along his back and locking her ankles behind his lower back. He lost any shred of self-control, and his cries mingled with hers until finally they lay in a sweaty, panting heap.

Coming back to his senses, he propped himself up on an elbow. "Am I crushing you?" he whispered, reaching down to brush the hair from her forehead.

Savannah wrapped her arms around him and squeezed. "Mmmmm, I like it."

Colin kissed her forehead and then her nose before placing a gentle kiss on her mouth. "Sorry that was so fast, but you do strange things to me."

"I don't think you're using the word 'fast' right because to me it felt like it took forever," she said with a soft laugh.

"You have no idea, sweetheart. But now that we've got the initial one out of the way, I'll be able to really take my time with you. Really make you feel good."

"I don't know how it could be better than that." Savannah rolled onto her side to face him.

Running his fingers through her hair and planting a soft kiss on her swollen lips, he said, "Challenge accepted."

And he kept his word. Twice.

Hours later, they lay in a tangled pile of arms and legs and sheets, Savannah's head resting on Colin's chest as he idly ran his fingers through her hair. Colin had imagined having Savannah in his bed many times since meeting her. But even in his best fantasy, he'd never imagined she would be as open or free as she'd been. She seemed to be holding nothing back, and it made Colin want her even more.

Savannah thought she must have died and gone to heaven. That maybe they'd been in a horrible car accident on the way home from the game and this was the afterlife, and she was OK with that.

"What ya thinking about, Red?" Colin asked softly, bringing Savannah out of her reverie.

"Mmmm hmmm." She sighed, snuggling in closer. "You."

"Hmm, tell me more," Colin said as he shifted to nuzzle her neck playfully.

"I was just thinking about how I feel like I know you so well, but really I don't know that much about your life outside of Zipped. Like how I had no idea you were in a basketball league."

Savannah playfully poked his side then squirmed in delight when he nipped at her earlobe in retaliation.

Colin's mind spun as he tried to decide how to respond. He didn't want to invent any more lies about his life, but this didn't feel like the time to come clean—not when she was so warm and soft snuggled up next to him.

"What would you like to know?" he asked, hoping to distract her by nibbling her neck.

"I don't know. Do you have any other siblings besides Chase?"

"I have an older sister and a younger sister who is still in high school," he answered carefully.

"I have a little sister who's in high school, too. In Fairfax. Where does your sister go?"

"She's here in D.C. My whole family lives in the District."

"Oh, you're one of those rare species that isn't a transplant? I thought that was a myth."

"Does this feel like a myth?" Colin teased as he took her hand and moved it to the hard ridge that had formed under the sheet.

"Again?!" Savannah asked with surprised laughter.

"What can I say? You have that effect on me," he said with a smile before covering her mouth with his.

Chapter 18

Savannah opened her eyes from a wonderful dream to an unfamiliar room with an unfamiliar, but not unpleasant, warmth surrounding her. Turning her head, she realized the warmth was coming from Colin's body curved around hers and that it hadn't been a dream at all. It had been very, very real. And perfect. She smiled as she snuggled deeper into Colin's arms. A little voice in her head kept asking her what would happen next, but she decided this was still pretend time and The Plan was still on hold. Colin murmured something in his sleep and tightened his hold around her, and Savannah closed her eyes and drifted back to sleep.

When she awoke again a few hours later, the early-morning sun was peeking through the window blinds and she was desperate for a glass of water. Carefully sliding out from under Colin's arm, she reached around on the floor for her clothes but couldn't find them, so she threw on Colin's T-shirt, which hung halfway down her thighs, and tiptoed out of his bedroom.

As she was crossing the living room toward the kitchen, the front door swung open and Chase walked in. Savannah froze, but when Chase saw her, he smiled calmly as if finding a half-naked woman in his living room at 6 a.m. on a Sunday was a regular occurrence. But then, maybe it was?

"Good morning," he said with a smile as he set down his duffel bag and tossed his keys onto the table by the door.

"Good morning," Savannah said and, not knowing what else do, continued into the kitchen but then stopped again because she realized she had no idea where the glasses were.

"Bottled water in the fridge," Chase called from the living room. "Help yourself."

Savannah opened the fridge, grabbed a bottle of water, and

was about to make a hasty retreat when Chase said, "Sarah, right? Colin's been hung up on you for a while. Finally gave in to his charms, huh?"

Savannah's insides turned to ice. Clearly, this was indeed a scene Chase was used to seeing—he couldn't even keep the names of all Colin's women straight.

"Yeah, something like that," she said.

Chase slipped a bulky camera bag from his shoulder and stifled a yawn. "So I take it he finally let you in on his little secret. I told him you'd be cool with it."

That icy cold feeling turned to a flush of heat, and she wanted to ask, "Which secret?" because Colin seemed to have so damn many, but Chase had already turned away, and a second later, he closed his bedroom door behind him.

She hurried back to Colin's room and gathered up her clothes as quietly as possible, desperate to get out of there before he woke up, before the tears that were building behind her eyes started to spill over. Pretend time was over.

When she reached the sidewalk, she realized she'd been so distracted on the cab ride over that she didn't know exactly where she was. But she was pretty sure Colin didn't live far from her place, so she picked a direction and started to walk, assuming she'd see something familiar soon. As she walked, she berated herself: "This is what happens when you deviate from The Plan! The Plan exists for a reason!"

Yesterday she'd convinced herself that she could do casual, that she could do temporary. But by the time she'd fallen asleep in his arms last night, she knew she was way past casual. She'd fallen hard for him, and if she was going to be honest, she'd started falling for him weeks ago. And the things he said, the way he acted had made Savannah think he was falling for her, too.

But now Chase had confirmed that Colin had indeed been keeping a secret from her. All her questions around his relationship with Crystal, plus that thing with the security guard and the woman at the stadium, made Savannah think it was something bigger than him just being a playboy—though that was bad enough. She started to wonder if maybe he'd bribed the guard at the game because money never seemed to be an issue for him. Aside from the fact that he never let her pay at Zipped, he wore a really nice watch that Savannah was fairly sure was a Tag Heuer, and she knew those weren't cheap. And his apartment building was one of those rehabbed historic buildings near the water. How could he possibly afford all that on a bartender's pay?

She came to a stop in front of her house, though she had no memory of navigating here. Now that she was home, the tears she'd held back started to fall, and she ran through the front door and up the stairs to Rayne's room. Savannah threw open the door to find Rayne sitting in bed typing on her laptop.

"Hey there party gir—" Rayne stopped when she saw Savannah's face. "What happened?"

"I'm such an idiot!" Savannah said before launching herself onto Rayne's bed. The trickle of tears turned to a river, and she just let them come.

Rayne stroked her hair for a few minutes before saying, "Nanna, tell me what's wrong. The text you sent me at 2 a.m. said *With Colin,* with a smiley face. What happened between then and now? And what happened to Steve? I thought you had a date with him, not Colin."

"I made a terrible mistake," Savannah said.

Rayne smiled. "Honey, I've told you all along that you should go for Colin. You never really were all that excited about Steve. And there's absolutely nothing wrong with revising your Plan a little bit."

"This isn't about The Plan. Well, maybe a little." Savannah sat up, and Rayne handed her a tissue, which Savannah used to wipe the tears from her face. She didn't know if she was ready to tell Rayne what she'd been thinking.

"So what happened?" Rayne asked again.

"Steve blew me off, and then Colin and I had this amazing day together. We went to the Nationals game and stayed for the concert afterward. And everything was so...perfect. And then we went back to his place."

Rayne was grinning. "And?"

"And the sex was perfect, too. Beyond perfect."

"So why do you look so miserable?" Rayne said, giving her a playful punch in the arm.

"I ran into Chase this morning when he was coming home from whatever trip he's been on." She saw a flicker of interest in Rayne's eyes but kept going. "And he called me Sarah. I thought Colin was being serious, I thought he really liked me, but clearly, I'm not the only woman in his life."

"Oh, honey. I think you're overreacting. I mean, Sarah isn't that different from Savannah. And you said yourself that Chase isn't the most reliable of people."

"He was completely unfazed to see me in his living room at six in the morning wearing one of Colin's shirts. It was obviously a familiar scene." She pounded a fist on the bed. "I knew I was being reckless, and I did it anyway."

Her eyes filled with tears again, and Rayne handed her another tissue and said, "Colin doesn't strike me as a player. I think he has real feelings for you. You should talk to him before you make up your mind."

"There's more," Savannah said, sniffling.

"What else is there?"

"He's been keeping some sort of secret from me," Savannah said. "I don't think he's who he says he is."

Rayne went still. "He's not married?"

"No, not that," Savannah said quickly. "I think...I mean, I'm not sure, but...I think he might be...selling drugs."

Rayne drew back in shock. "Colin? Drugs? No! What makes you say that?"

"Think about it: He pays for our food and drinks all the time, like it's no big deal. Plus, he has these weird conversations with Crystal over at Sweet Happens, and she looks seriously strung-out until he agrees to get something for her. And he handed something to the security guard to get him to let us into the baseball stadium yesterday, but he purposely made sure I didn't see it, and I'm not sure if it was cash or...something else."

"Savannah, I think you're—"

"And we ran into this woman at the game. He said she was some kind of 'business associate,' and I heard them talking about 'missing inventory,' and Colin was really rattled. And then this morning, Chase said he was glad I was cool with Colin's secret."

Rayne was silent for a moment, looking stunned. Finally she said, "I did worry that he was going to go broke feeding both of us and buying us drinks. But drugs?" She looked up at Savannah. "Like, what? Pot?"

"I have no idea. Pot maybe, cocaine—could be anything!" She twisted up a handful of Rayne's bedspread, and the enormity of it all finally hit her.

"I could lose my job," she said. "The foundation has a zero-tolerance policy for drug use."

"But you're not using drugs," Rayne protested.

"I'm pretty sure the policy extends to dating a drug dealer." Her shoulders sagged. "Oh god, Rayney, how did I ever let this happen?"

Rayne put her arm around Savannah's shoulders. "What do you want to do now?" she asked. "What can I do to help?"

"I don't know. Distract me? I need to take a shower, but then maybe we can go out to breakfast or something?"

"You've got it," Rayne said with a smile. "I'll meet you downstairs whenever you're ready."

Chapter 19

Colin opened his eyes and glanced at the alarm clock by the bed. It was a little after eight. Then he rolled over to snuggle up to Savannah, but she wasn't there. Reaching over the side of the bed for his clothes, he noticed that her clothes were gone, and there was an unopened bottle of water on his dresser.

He was puzzled and more than a little disappointed that she'd left without waking him. Last night had been amazing, and it seemed like she agreed, too. He thought he'd finally gotten a toehold against the wall of The Plan. Maybe she'd gone out to get them coffee and donuts...?

He picked his pants off the floor, dug out his cell phone, and dialed Savannah, but it went straight to voicemail. At the beep, he said, "Hey, Red. Just woke up and saw you were gone. Give me a call, OK?"

As he dropped the phone onto the bed and pulled on sweats and a T-shirt, he started to get a sinking feeling. Maybe it had all been too fast for her after all? Maybe the morning light had brought regrets?

He picked up the bottle of water and drank it down in one long swallow. Then he headed to the kitchen to throw the bottle away and noticed Chase's duffel bag by the door. He briefly wondered when his brother had come in but was too absorbed in trying to figure out what to do next to even think about what Chase might have heard going on last night.

Colin tried Savannah's cell again, and again, it went straight to voicemail. So he sent her a text: *Hey, missed you this morning. Call me* followed by a kiss emoji.

He took a long, hot shower and went over the events of the previous day—and night—and couldn't figure out any reason for Savannah to take off, other than getting cold feet over that ridiculous Plan of hers. He reminded himself that he'd known this would take more patience than he was used to, but he was determined to talk to her. And the sooner, the better.

When he walked out of his room with his hair still wet from the shower, he found Chase sprawled on the couch channel surfing.

"Yo!" Chase said without taking his eyes from the TV.

"Hey. When did you get back?" Colin asked.

"Early this morning."

"Cool. Well, I'll catch you later." Colin headed for the door, thinking he'd go to Savannah's place and take her out for brunch somewhere fancy, thinking that maybe now was the time to tell her that he didn't just work at Zipped, he owned it.

"Oh hey!" Chase said, sitting up and looking at Colin for the first time. "I met your friend this morning when I got in. The chick you've been hung up on for weeks. Sarah? Way to seal that deal, bro."

Chase held out his fist for a bump with Colin, who kept his hands at his sides.

"Savannah," Colin said as a sick feeling started to creep through his body.

"Huh?"

"Her name is Savannah. What time did you see her?"

"6 maybe? And I don't think that's her name. She didn't correct me when I called her Sarah."

Colin wanted to vomit. Or punch Chase. Instead he turned toward the door with renewed urgency.

"You are a serious asshole," Colin said.

"I should have stuck with 'Sunshine,' huh?" Chase said, still not getting the seriousness of the situation. "Relax, bro. I'm sure you can make everything right...as rain." He snapped his fingers. "That's her name—Rayne! That hot chick from the bar, right?"

Colin was halfway down the hall, but he suddenly turned back. "Did you say anything else to her this morning?"

Chase had gone back to channel surfing, but he couldn't miss the intensity in Colin's voice, so he set the remote down and thought about it. "Maybe."

"Such as?"

Chase actually looked concerned, though whether it was for Savannah or his own skin, Colin couldn't say.

"You didn't tell her, did you?" Chase asked.

"Tell her what?" Colin was trying to keep himself from shouting.

"About not just being a bartender at Zipped?"

Colin stared at him wildly, and Chase said, "How could I know? I was just trying to make conversation—you know, make her feel at home. I know how hot you've been for her."

"Chase! Tell me exactly what you said."

"I just said I assumed you had told her the truth and that everything was cool. But you didn't, did you?"

"No, I didn't. And now she thinks I've been lying to her."

"Well, bro, you have."

"Shut up, Chase."

"Look, I know you've been playing out some fairy-tale fantasy about having a girl fall in love with you for who you are instead of your money, but she's going to have to know sometime. And the longer you wait, the worse it will be. Trust me, chicks don't get over that stuff very easily."

"I can't believe you of all people are giving me relationship advice. You've never been with a woman for more than a month."

Chase smiled. "Not true. There was this woman in Bali.... Best six weeks of my life."

Colin rolled his eyes, then ran out the front door and let it slam shut behind him.

Colin tried calling Savannah as he walked, but the call again went straight to voicemail. When he got to her house, he took the porch steps two at a time and banged on the door. When he got no response, he knocked again, louder. Finally a woman in yoga pants and tank top yanked the door open.

"We don't want whatever you're selling," she said and immediately started to close the door.

"Wait!" Colin said. "I'm looking for Savannah."

"She's not here."

He stared at the woman, knowing Savannah and Rayne had talked about her before, racking his brain for her name, and felt a pang of empathy for Chase that was quickly replaced with anger.

"Carol, right?" To his relief, the woman nodded, though warily. "Do you know where Savannah is or when she'll be back?"

Carol stared at him for several seconds, so he added, "I need to talk to her about something, and it's really, really important."

Carol shrugged. "I guess you're too cute to be a stalker. She and Rayne went out to brunch a couple of hours ago. But Savannah didn't look too good." She paused and frowned at Colin. "Wait...did you do that?"

Colin sighed. "Maybe? Probably. But it's a big misunderstanding. Which is why I need to find her as soon as possible."

"I don't know where they went, so there's not much more I can do for you." Carol started to close the door again.

"Do you mind if I wait on the porch?"

"Knock yourself out," she said.

Chapter 20

"Ugh, I'm stuffed," Savannah said, pushing away the last bites of her Belgian waffle.

"Already? After only eating sixty percent of the brunch menu?" Rayne teased as she sipped the tea that she'd switched to when Savannah had ordered her second mocha latte.

"I'm self-medicating with carbs and sugar," Savannah said.

"Has it helped any?"

"Well, now I can tell myself the sick feeling in my stomach is just from the food."

"That's something, at least," Rayne said, setting down her cup. "Have you turned your phone on yet?"

"No, but it doesn't matter. I don't want to talk to him."

"I think you should. Maybe there's an innocent explanation—"

"No." Savannah cut her off and sat up straight. "This is good actually. He's doesn't fit The Plan. And I knew that the whole time. But I was having fun, and so I shut off my brain for the day. And this is the consequence." She glanced out the window. "It's just as well it happened now, before things went further."

Fresh tears pricked at the backs of her eyes as images of exactly how far it had gone flashed through her mind. Taking a deep breath and squaring her shoulders, she shook the images from her mind.

"Actually the timing's perfect," she said. "The foundation's donor event is only two weeks away, and I still have a ton of work to do on it. He would have just been a distraction."

"Savannah—"

"Let's get out of here. I've got to do laundry and get ready for the week."

They turned the corner onto their street, and Savannah stopped short when she saw Colin sitting on the porch steps. As soon as he saw her, he got up. He didn't know what to expect, but his heart sank when she squared her shoulders and flipped her hair back, readying herself for battle.

She and Rayne starting walking again and met him at the end of the pathway onto the sidewalk. He nodded toward Rayne without taking his eyes off Savannah. "Hey, Rayne."

"Hey, Colin," Rayne said softly, glancing from him to Savannah, who was staring at Colin stone-faced.

"Hey, Red," Colin said with a hopeful smile.

Her green eyes flashed with emotion briefly before going blank again, and he felt like he'd been kicked in the gut.

Savannah glanced away from Colin and shoved her hands in her pockets as Rayne hurried into the house.

Colin cleared his throat. "Chase told me what he said this morning. He's a total idiot when it comes to names. I swear it's some kind of ADD. There is no Sarah. And—"

"You don't owe me any explanation," Savannah said, finally looking at him.

"I do, though. Yesterday was perfect. Last night was amazing. Please don't let Chase's foot-in-mouth disease ruin it, ruin us." His eyes were full of a concern that seemed genuine.

"It doesn't matter," Savannah said, looking away again.

"Of course it matters!"

He had envisioned this conversation going a lot of ways, but he'd never pictured her so withdrawn. So...*still*. This was so much worse.

"Savannah, please," he begged again and stepped to the left to try to get in her line of vision, but she busied herself tying up her hair to avoid looking at him. "Listen to me. There's only you. Since the first time I saw you on that porch," he said gesturing toward the house, "there's only ever been you."

Savannah finally looked into Colin's eyes, and he thought he could see her resolve starting to melt. But then she took a deep breath and a step back and said, "Why should I believe you? I barely know you."

"Really? I feel like we know each other pretty well, especially after last night," Colin said, hoping to reconnect with her a little.

"Yesterday was pretend."

He was stunned. "Nothing about yesterday was pretend!" He reached out to put his hand on her arm, but she pulled away.

"It was all make-believe," she said. "Everything between us has been an act."

"That's not true," he said, and a pang of guilt cut through him because he knew that technically she had a point, though emotionally Colin believed everything between them was completely authentic. "I was going to tell you. I just wanted you to get to know me first."

"Tell me what?" She was watching him now with a mix of fear and eagerness, and Colin suddenly realized that Chase hadn't told her the nature of his secret and it was still up to him to do that.

When he took too long to answer, she said, "I knew you'd been hiding something from me. I knew it all along, but I ignored it."

"I am seriously going to break Chase's jaw so he can never say another stupid thing."

She was still watching him intently. "What's going on between you and Crystal?"

"Crystal? She and I aren't...we're just...we're friends." Shit. Colin knew he sounded like he was lying, but he was not prepared to explain his involvement with Crystal right now.

Savannah said nothing.

"Crystal and I have a...uh...business deal. But trust me, honey, when I say there is absolutely nothing romantic between us. But it's just not my place to tell you Crystal's business."

"And what about at the ballpark yesterday?" Savannah said. "How did you convince that security guard to let us in?"

Colin thought about telling her the truth—that his family owned a concession stand at the stadium and he'd shown the guy his ID to get inside. But he really didn't think it would help if he started unfolding all the secrets bit by bit in the middle of the sidewalk. If he could get her alone, get her to calm down, he could tell her everything and it wouldn't end in her refusing to talk to him ever again.

Savannah read the panic in his eyes and decided to press her advantage. "How do you know him again?"

"What—now you think I'm dating the security guard, too?" Colin asked, trying to distract her and buy himself some time.

"Are you? Is that what you're hiding? That you go both ways?"

"No, but after the insanity of this conversation I might consider switching teams."

"Maybe you should!" Savannah yelled, not really knowing what she was saying but realizing that if she walked away now, it would truly be over.

"Savannah, what are we even talking about?" Colin softened his voice and took a step toward her. "How did we go from Chase's stupid comment to questioning my sexual orientation?"

Savannah exhaled and shook her head, suddenly feeling so worn out and wanting to just crawl into bed and cry alone. "Have you been lying to me all along? Is there anything that's true?"

Colin felt like she'd stabbed him right through the heart. "Savannah, sweetheart, please. The important stuff, our connection, my feelings for you, they're as real as it gets." He took a step toward her, desperate to touch her.

But she took a step back, shoulders hunched and arms crossed in front of her chest in a self-protective stance. "So that means everything else, everything about your actual life, was a lie then, right?"

"No! No, I don't mean that." Colin raked his hands through his hair in frustration, feeling everything slipping out of his control. "Look, I'll tell you everything you want to know about me and even stuff you probably don't want to know. Just please, give me that chance. Let's go someplace a little more private, and we can talk as long as you want."

Sensing a softening in her features, Colin reached out and touched the back of her hand. She looked down at her hand for a moment then pulled back.

"No, I'm not falling for that," she said. "I'm not getting sucked in by your charm again. Say what you need to right here. Or just forget it."

"Savannah, come on." Colin felt his frustration reaching a boiling point. She was making this harder than it had to be. "I don't want to do this on a sidewalk in the middle of Capitol Hill. Be reasonable."

"Why not? Is it because what you're hiding is illegal?"

"What?" Colin was thoroughly confused. "No! No, of course not. Let's just go back to my place and I'll explain everything."

But she kept that watchful gaze on him and said in a level voice, "Are you a drug dealer?"

"Am I WHAT?" Colin said, caught completely off guard.

"It all makes sense—the nice apartment, the meals and drinks you've been buying me and Rayne, your secret connections all over town. Your fancy watch."

He looked down at his watch, an extremely generous gift from his mother. It was way fancier than anything he would normally wear, but he was sentimental about it. He started to give Savannah the response he gave anyone who pointed out his watch—that it was a knock-off—but stopped himself before he lied to her again.

"Wow," he said. He felt like he'd been hit with a bucket of ice water, and the tenuous hold he'd had on his emotions started to fray. "After everything, after all the time we've spent together, that's what you think of me? That I'm a freaking drug dealer?"

He turned and walked a few paces away from her before stopping and letting out a short, humorless laugh. "I have to admit, I did not see that coming. I would have preferred a condescending 'just a bartender' brush-off."

She looked stung by the last remark.

"You know what?" he said as he felt that frayed line snap. "That's just fine. You want to believe I'm a drug dealer? Fine. FINE! Because you know what I just realized? You're nuts!"

Colin wanted to feel satisfaction at the hurt that flickered across her face, but he didn't. Nothing about this felt good.

"You and your ridiculous Plan and your green eyes and...and...

I don't need it! I. Don't. Need. It."

He wanted to kick something, he wanted to break something, but most of all, he wished he'd never seen her twirling on her porch that morning. His plan to counteract her Plan had been a disaster, and he should have swallowed his pride and moved on long ago.

He took a deep breath and raked his hands through his already messy hair. "You have yourself a nice life, Red."

Then he turned and, shoving his hands deep in his pockets to stop himself from punching a tree, stalked toward home.

Savannah didn't move a single muscle until he had turned the corner and was out of sight. Then she sank down on the bottom steps and laid her head on her knees and cried harder than she'd cried in years. Within minutes, Rayne's arms were around her. Savannah leaned against her friend and let herself wallow for a moment longer before taking a deep breath and sitting up straight. Wiping her eyes, she gave Rayne a rueful smile.

"So that's done," she said with a weak attempt at a laugh.

"Sweetie, I think you should—"

"No, no. I'm fine. It's how it has to be."

"Did you ask him if he was a drug dealer?"

Savannah nodded.

"And?"

"He got super pissed. But he also didn't exactly deny it. So I guess that tells me what I need to know."

"Not necessarily! It's a pretty big leap."

"Whose side are you on?!" Savannah said, getting to her feet.

"Yours, of course! But I'm just saying—"

"No, please don't say anything. I'm done talking about this." Savannah said. "I have no time for self-pity or regret. I need to focus on my job. I have to make this event amazing, the best my boss has ever seen. I have to at least have that."

She walked into the house while making a mental list of everything she needed to do that day and pulling her hair into a severe bun, and although she didn't feel any better, she at least felt a little more in control.

Chapter 21

For the next week, Savannah threw herself into her work, believing that total absorption in her event's minutia was the only salve for her broken heart. She started wearing a rubber band on her wrist, and every time she caught herself thinking about Colin or missing him, she'd snap it in a lame attempt at behavior modification.

To complete her cone of concentration, she suspended all her online dating profiles and networking group memberships so she didn't have to wade through a bunch of email messages every day. And she'd taken to getting to the office early and staying late.

Thursday afternoon at 5:15, the beeping of her cell phone pulled her attention away from her master spreadsheet. It was a message from Rayne.

Hey stranger! Haven't seen you all week. Meet me for happy hour?! We can go anywhere you want, even another neighborhood.

Savannah quickly typed back, *Can't. Too much work.* Then she dropped the phone back into her bag and returned to her spreadsheet. But the beeping of new messages wore her down, and she pulled it out again.

Rayne said, *I need proof of life. Beyond random takeout containers in the kitchen trash.*

Isn't this conversation proof of life?

This could be your kidnapper pretending to be you to give himself more time to sell you into sex slavery.

Savannah laughed but didn't respond because she didn't want to encourage a long texting conversation. A few minutes later, her phone beeped again.

That's it! I'm calling the police.

With an amused sigh, she held the phone up and took a

selfie, making sure to look as tired and annoyed as possible. She sent it to Rayne and typed, *Proof of life. And if you leave me alone, I'll try to be home by 9 and we can have a drink on the porch.*

I'll take what I can get.

Savannah wanted to ask if Rayne was going to Zipped for trivia night and earned herself a snap of the rubber band.

All week Colin had tried and failed to stop himself from looking up every time the door opened, thinking Savannah would walk through. Now, on trivia night, it was worse than it had been all week. His pulse quickened every time a woman with long dark hair came through the door, and he realized that he'd unconsciously spent the whole week thinking that trivia night would be what brought her back through that door. She would apologize for accusing him of being a womanizer and a drug dealer, he'd tell her the truth about his family, they'd kiss in the middle of the bar, and everyone would applaud.

Now that trivia night was here, he realized how stupid he'd been. But when the door opened a minute later and Rayne walked in, his heart did an extra beat as he looked past her to see if Savannah was there.

"Sorry, just me," Rayne said, sliding onto a stool and trying to casually look around the bar for Chase.

"Sorry, just me," Colin said with a slight smile.

Rayne was embarrassed, but she laughed. Then she leaned forward and dropped her voice to a near-whisper. "So," she said, "do you really know Molly?"

Colin went cold, and he stared at her without humor. He should have known Savannah would tell Rayne about her suspicions—and Rayne would believe her.

"Do you even know what Molly is?" he asked.

"It's the stuff all the kids are into now—like…ecstasy? And it's in that Miley Cyrus song, right?"

Colin leaned toward her. "Do us both a favor and never talk about Molly again." Then he grabbed a bottle of gin and started fixing a drink.

Rayne's smile faltered. "Fair enough."

"It's bad enough that Savannah thinks I'm a drug dealer," Colin said as he set a gin and tonic in front of Rayne. "I'd rather not have it spread throughout the whole neighborhood." He paused then, suddenly picturing the shit storm that would happen if he parents got wind of a rumor like that.

"I don't believe you're a drug dealer." She took a sip of the drink and sighed. "Besides, why would you need drugs when you can make drinks like this?"

He shot her a look of annoyance, then softened. Rayne wasn't the enemy.

"Thanks for the vote of confidence, but it doesn't really matter at this point. Savannah believes I'm a dealer—and a womanizer. And frankly, I'd rather not waste my time on a woman who has such a low opinion of me."

Rayne looked taken aback, but she didn't respond, and for the next half-hour, Colin moved around the bar serving drinks and picking up dirty dishes. The place was starting to fill up with couples and larger groups coming in for trivia night. But he could feel her watching him as he went about his work. Finally, he set a paper cone of fries and an array of dipping sauces in front of her.

Rayne ignored the food and said, "She's really upset about all this. And now she's wrapped herself up in this work project, and I haven't even seen her in days."

"Am I supposed to care?" Colin said, his anger getting the better of him. "She brought this on herself with that idiotic plan of hers. If it wasn't for her Plan, I never would have had to come up with my stupid plan. And I wouldn't have had to lie about who I am."

Rayne looked at him in open-mouthed surprise, and he wished he could bite back his words. He abruptly picked up a rag from the edge of the bar and threw it toward a dish bin, and suppressing the urge to yell in frustration, walked back toward his office. Rayne jumped up and ran down the bar, catching up with at the doorway.

"What plan?" she said.

Colin turned, intending to ignore her, and almost crashed into

Diana as she came through the doorway with a tray of food held high. She looked from Colin to Rayne and said with annoyance, "We're all out of catfish nuggets," and walked on.

Colin scrubbed his face in frustration before glancing at Rayne, knowing he wasn't getting out of this.

"I knew you had an ulterior motive with the catfish nuggets! But what was the lie?" She paused then her eyes went wide. "Where those guys all fakes that you got to ask her out to make sure none of them worked out?"

Colin rolled his eyes in exasperation.

"You might as well tell her," Diana said as she walked by again on her way back to the kitchen. "It's all gone to hell anyway. I should've put money on it."

"She's right. You should definitely tell me." Rayne finally let go of his arm but kept staring at him, her hands on her hips.

"Fine!" he said. "I thought that if I showed her that these guys—the ones who fit her Plan—were no good for her, she'd see that I *was* right for her, even though I was just a bartender. And then she'd see that her whole plan was ridiculous, and she could stop pretending there wasn't a spark between us."

As soon as he said it, his strategy sounded idiotic and immature. And some part of him had known that was the case all along.

"So you came up with a plan to counteract her Plan?" Rayne said slowly and broke into a smile. "You guys might be even better suited to each other than I thought."

Colin frowned, but when Rayne started to laugh, he couldn't resist smiling. "Yeah, it was pretty lame. But I couldn't think of anything else. That freaking Plan of hers—where the hell did it come from anyway?"

"She's always had some kind of plan for her life," Rayne said. "Her dad told me once that instead of playing house, she used to play CEO and have staff meetings with her stuffed animals."

"I can totally picture that," Colin said, smiling. "But that's a far cry from only dating men who fit some arbitrary standard and having every minute of your life planned like you're some sort of robot."

"Yes," Rayne said, hesitating slightly before continuing. "But there's more to the story. There's a reason for the plan. Or at least a cause."

A customer motioned to Colin from the bar. He looked around and realized that the place was packed and he only had a few minutes before the trivia game was supposed to start.

"I have to get back to work," he said. "And your fries are getting cold."

He went over to the customer and poured him a beer, then he picked up the remote and flipped through the channels until the trivia screen came up. He met Rayne back at her seat just as the hostess grabbed the mic and started going over the rules.

Rayne dipped a fry into the honey mustard sauce and popped it into her mouth. "Mmmmmm, this is delicious," she said.

"Thanks," he said as he brought her another gin and tonic. "Look, I really appreciate you coming in here and trying to help out, but I've had enough of the plans and the games. I'm just going to move on."

"Oh, don't do that!" Rayne said. "I mean, you guys are so great together. She just needs some time."

"And what about me? How long am I supposed to wait around hoping she comes to her senses and realizes I'm not a low-life drug dealer?" He glanced around, hoping no one had heard that last part over all the commotion in the bar.

"There was a guy—in college," Rayne blurted out.

Colin looked at her and raised an eyebrow. Rayne glanced around, suddenly afraid that Savannah might be standing behind her. She hadn't wanted to tell Colin, but Savannah likely never would. And Rayne couldn't sit idly by and let her friend lose a man she was obviously so crazy about and who was so perfect for her.

Rayne hunched closer to the bar so she wouldn't have to raise her voice to be heard, and Colin leaned toward her.

"When Savannah got to college," Rayne said, "she had her entire education planned out semester by semester through getting an MA in public administration. First semester of sophomore year, she was right on track—honor roll, club president, the whole deal. Then she met Jake. He was a junior and an art major. So he's all tortured and dramatic and intense and counter-culture in a way that Savannah had never experienced. The fact that he was gorgeous and sexy as hell didn't hurt either."

Colin winced, but she kept going. "Jake set his sights on her and wooed her with sidewalk murals and terrible poetry, and pretty soon she was head over heels. But he was super needy, and once she was in, he wanted all her attention and all her time. And she gave it to him. Instead of going home for the holiday break, she moved into his off-campus group house. She wouldn't even go home on Christmas Day, and it's only a thirty-five-minute drive!"

Rayne took a long sip of her drink before continuing. "Her parents totally flipped out, but they couldn't get her to talk to them, so they stopped sending her money to live on. And when that didn't get any reaction, they threatened to stop paying tuition. She was acting so bizarre that we were wondering if she was on drugs or if she'd joined a cult. It was all so extreme and intense and so…not like her."

Rayne stopped talking, suddenly seeing the similarities between then and now, only in reverse: Savannah was so scared of repeating those mistakes that she was acting just as extreme in shutting everyone out and throwing herself into her work.

"So how did it all end?" Colin asked, picking at a nick in the bar, trying not to let this story make him feel bad for Savannah. "Because obviously she got it together at some point."

"She failed most of her classes that fall and missed registration for spring semester, so she was taking these random, leftover classes, like archery and remedial math, and she'd also lost her job so she was flat broke. Everything in her life was a disaster, but all she seemed to care about was Jake. Then one day she comes home and finds him naked with some interpretive dance major."

"I could have seen that coming," Colin said with a shake of his head.

"I know, right?! And he doesn't try to hide it or apologize

and instead says that she'd been neglecting him and he needed company, and she should just loosen up and join them—"

"Stop! I get the picture."

"That snapped her out of it. She went straight to her parents' house, withdrew from GW for the semester, stayed in Fairfax, got a job, and came up with The Plan. She took a double course load over the summer and hasn't strayed from The Plan since."

"Until me," Colin said.

"Everyone knows you can't pick your husband based on a random list of checkboxes. But she doesn't trust her instincts when it comes to men. The Plan is her refuge. And it's served her really, really well. Until now."

Colin got called away by another customer, and Rayne was suddenly tired of being jostled by all the people squeezed around the bar laughing and talking. And she was just tired in general. Fixing things between Savannah and Colin was going to be harder than she thought, and her heart sank at the notion that it might not even be possible. But something Colin had said earlier still nagged at her.

She watched as the waiters and waitresses came to him with drink orders and realized that he looked totally at home—and in charge. They seemed to look up to him, defer to him even, though he was on friendly terms with all of them. And then she realized that she'd never seen a manager in the place.

Rayne finally caught his eye, and he came over.

"I need to settle my tab," she said. "I'm hoping to meet up with Savannah at home."

"On the house," he said.

She wanted to argue about the bill, but he was already turning away. "Wait!" she called and almost reached over the bar to grab him by the sleeve. "What you said earlier, about lying about who you are?"

Diana came up and said something to him, and he nodded.

"I'm kind of busy now," he said to Rayne as he started grabbing clean glasses from under the bar. "Maybe some other time."

Later that night, Savannah and Rayne sat on the porch swing with a bottle of wine and a box of mini cupcakes from Sweet Happens between them.

"So. You look like hell," Rayne said, licking chocolate frosting off her fingers.

"Gee, thanks." Savannah had been all sharp edges and grumpy noises since she'd gotten home.

"I'm just saying, it can't be productive to run yourself this ragged."

"I have no choice. I have so much to prove and my concentration is for shit this week and I can't sleep anyway, so I might as well be working."

"Because of Colin?"

Savannah gave her a look dripping with sarcasm. "No, because I'm worried about the ozone layer."

Rayne laughed softly. "You should be worried about it. But let me handle that while you figure out this Colin thing."

"There's nothing to figure out. I knew better, but I let things get out of hand and this is the price I have to pay. I thought work would distract me, and it does to a point but…" She trailed off, suddenly engrossed in studying the wine in her glass.

"But you miss him."

Savannah rolled her eyes in response. "Yeah, fine, I miss him. Are you happy?"

"No, I'm not."

"I never should have slept with him," Savannah said. "Maybe we'd still be friends now."

Rayne refilled her wine glass. "You don't really think he's a drug dealer, do you?"

Savannah sighed. "I don't know. Maybe. He's been lying to me about something. That's all I know for sure."

"It could be something perfectly harmless—or just embarrassing," Rayne said. "Like, maybe he collects Beanie Babies or listens to barbershop music. Or eats at chain restaurants."

Ignoring the joke, Savannah picked up her half-eaten cupcake and got to her feet. "My event is next Saturday, and I've got to meet with the caterers first thing tomorrow, so I'm going to call it a night."

Rayne nodded, but as Savannah opened the door to the house, Rayne asked, "What did you say Colin's last name was?"

"Allison," Savannah said and closed the door behind her.

Chapter 22

For the next several days, Savannah's whole world revolved around work and sleep. She rarely saw Rayne and then only in passing. As much as she wanted to just be left alone for a while, by Thursday she was tired of thinking about Colin and tired of missing Rayne. She had everything in order for the event Saturday night and felt justified in taking the evening off.

She dug her phone out of her bag and sent Rayne a text. *Hey you. Wanna do happy hour or something tonight?*

The response came almost immediately. *Yes. You name the place and time, I'll be there.*

Savannah felt a lump form in her throat. She didn't deserve Rayne. *I heard there's a new wine bar on 7th. Want to go there? 6:00?*

See you at 6! Rayne responded, followed by a smiley face emoji and a clapping emoji.

Savannah smiled as she put her phone away and finally started to feel a little less miserable.

At 6:00 on the dot, Savannah walked into Balance&Bite. The polished concrete floor and the high ceilings with exposed metal beams were warmed up with wood planking on the walls and bar, creating an environment that was both rustic and elegant. She saw Rayne sitting at a high two-person table near floor-to-ceiling windows overlooking tree-lined D Street. They were among a handful of customers, but the bar had only been open a few days and Savannah knew that within weeks it would impossible to find a table at happy hour.

"Wow, this place is swanky!" she said as she got to the table.

Rayne slid off her chair and pulled Savannah into a hug, which Savannah returned fiercely. After a few seconds, Rayne finally let go and said, "I know. Because if there was one thing this city was missing, it was another fancy wine bar."

Savannah laughed as she settled herself into her chair. "We're going to have to up our game if we want to fit in."

After they had reviewed the tiny chalkboard happy hour menu on their table and ordered a flight of wines and a Mediterranean tasting plate, Savannah looked at Rayne and said, "This is...nice. Thanks for meeting me."

"Of course!"

Their waiter arrived with their wine and food, and when he walked away, Savannah said, "I swear that guy looks just like one of the waiters at Zipped."

Rayne craned around in her chair to take another look. "Yeah, he does seem kinda familiar. Come to think of it, I think I saw him there last week."

Savannah popped an olive in her mouth and tried to sound casual. "You were at Zipped last week?"

Rayne swiveled back around to face Savannah, and her cheeks had gone a little pink. "Yeah. I was kinda hoping to run into Chase there on trivia night."

"Rayney, we talked about this."

"I know, I know. But you've been so busy and I felt like getting out. And he's fun to talk to. It didn't matter anyway because he wasn't there."

Savannah spread some hummus on a square of toasted flat bread and tried to ignore the way Rayne was staring at her.

"Colin was there, though," Rayne said.

"Makes sense," Savannah said. "Thursday is a busy night."

Rayne took a sip of her wine, her eyes still on Savannah. "I think he's every bit as upset as you are."

Savannah didn't respond. Instead, she gazed out the window at the trees swaying slightly in the breeze.

"Colin is not Jake," Rayne said. "And this is not college."

Savannah turned to her in surprise and opened her mouth to argue, but Rayne held up a hand to stop her.

"I've given this a lot of thought so just hear me out," she said. "What happened in college was awful, but you were nineteen years old. And you still pulled yourself back together, and you are stronger and smarter for it. Your plan is mostly solid, except for the life partner part. That's total crap. You can't control love like that."

"Rayne, please—" Savannah said, but Rayne leaned toward her across the table and kept going.

"A person's job doesn't tell you if he's going to make you feel loved and valuable and safe. Whether he wears a suit to work or jeans and a T-shirt is not a predictor of how easily he makes you laugh or how you get butterflies in your stomach when you see him. Your whole list is an attempt to control something that isn't controllable. Colin is honest and caring and funny, and he's crazy about you. Don't let Jake take this away from you, too."

Savannah was stunned. Rayne wasn't one for making big impassioned speeches, and she had just reinforced the fears that had been haunting Savannah—that Colin was much more than a fling and she was close to fucking up everything. Tears slid down her cheeks, and she dropped her head into her hands. A moment later, her shoulders started to tremble.

"Oh! Oh no! Oh, I'm sorry I yelled at you!" Rayne cried, jumping up to put her arm around Savannah. "I was too mean, wasn't I? And I shouldn't have done it in public! I'm so sorry, sweetie!"

Savannah slowly lifted her head to show that, despite the tears, she was also laughing.

"Oh shit, you're having a nervous breakdown!" Rayne said. "What do I do?"

At Rayne's reaction, Savannah started laughing harder, which made Rayne look even more panicked.

Savannah finally managed to choke out, "Oh my god, Rayne. You should see your face!"

Rayne stepped back with her hands on her hips. "What the hell is wrong with you?"

"I'm sorry!" Savannah said, still shaking with laughter. "I don't know what happened, but suddenly it felt like this huge weight was lifted and I realized that for you to give a speech like that it must be serious and...I don't know! It all just seemed really, really funny all of a sudden."

She stopped to catch her breath and wipe away the tears. "Maybe I am losing it." And then she started to giggle again, and after a second, Rayne joined in and they collapsed against each other, overcome with laughter.

After a few minutes, Rayne finally pulled back. "We're making a scene," she whispered, and Savannah looked over to see several customers watching them.

Rayne went back to her seat, and the waiter stopped by and asked if they'd like to see a dinner menu. Savannah looked at Rayne, who shrugged, and so Savannah said sure. As the waiter was about to leave, she said to him, "You look really familiar. Do you by any chance work at a bar called Zipped?"

The guy smiled. He had blond hair cut short, pale blue eyes, and a weight-lifter's muscular arms. "I thought I'd seen you two in there," he said. "I'm just helping out here until things take off. Though to tell you the truth," he leaned in close, "I'd just as soon switch to this place full-time. I think the tips will be better here. Different clientele, know what I mean?"

He tucked his pen behind his ear and added, "But that's up to Colin, of course," before heading over to another table.

"Why would Colin have a say in where else his waiters work?" Savannah said.

"So you never googled Colin, huh?"

Savannah looked embarrassed. "It didn't occur to me because we weren't dating, and then after everything…well, I just didn't want to know."

"Well, I did," Rayne said. "After you told me his last name was Allison, I did some checking around. I've worked with reporters long enough that I know how to do some sleuthing of my own. Allison Inc. owns Zipped, and they own this bar, too. In fact, they run most of the profitable bars and restaurants in this town. They're like the mafia of the restaurant industry."

"Are you saying Colin is one of those Allisons? But why would he lie—" Savannah halted in midsentence because Rayne's eyes had gone wide and she was staring at something behind Savannah.

Savannah slowly turned to see Chase walking toward them.

"Well, this place has just gotten a whole lot classier," he said with a smile. "Hello, Rayne. Hello, *Savannah*."

"Fancy meeting you here," Rayne said, smiling at him as she fidgeted with the stem of her wine glass.

"Fancy indeed," Chase said, grinning back at her. "We're meeting our parents for dinner. Is Colin here yet?"

Savannah's face went white, and she shook her head no.

"Weird. I'm never the first one to show up for a family event. Maybe he and Jess are coming over together."

Savannah felt a rush of heat go through her body. Shit! Not only was she going to have to see Colin, but he was bringing a date. She caught Rayne's eye and tilted her head toward the door, the universal sign for *Let's get the hell out of here*.

But Rayne returned her plea with a plea of her own and a slight nod toward Chase. Savannah was seriously debating grabbing her bag and leaving, regardless of how rude that looked, when a woman came walking toward them.

"Hey, bro, don't hassle the customers," she said to Chase.

It was Jessica, the manager of the Lounge, the woman who'd been so kind to Savannah after her disastrous date with Ryan. Jessica recognized her in the same instant.

"Hey!" she said. "Savannah, right?"

"Yes, I can't believe you remembered."

"Not all Allisons are mentally challenged when it comes to names," Jessica said with a pointed look at Chase. "And Colin has mentioned you a time or two," she added with a twinkle in her eye that seemed very familiar.

Savannah suddenly noticed the family resemblance and registered the fact that Jessica had just lumped herself in with the Allisons.

"Wait—you guys are related?" she asked.

"Jess is my baby sister," Chase said.

"I hate when you call me that."

"What's wrong with 'sister'?" he asked, feigning innocence.

She rolled her eyes. "See what I have to deal with?" she said to Rayne and Savannah. Turning back to Chase, she said, "So where's the man of the hour?"

"Colin?" Chase said, helping himself to a hunk of feta from the plate on the table. "Putting the finishing touches on his PowerPoint slides probably. But he'd better hurry up—I'm starving."

The waiter showed up with the menus, but Savannah said, "We changed our minds. We won't be having dinner." Then she got to her feet and slung her bag over her shoulder.

"It was nice seeing you again, Jessica," she said. "And you, too, Chase."

Rayne slid out of her chair reluctantly. "Maybe I'll see you around," she said to Chase.

He smiled. "Hope so."

Savannah was resisting the urge to grab Rayne by the hand and drag her to the door, and she spun around so fast that she bumped right into Colin. He immediately took a step back. He was wearing his usual jeans, but today he had on a white button-down shirt that was open at the throat and a wide leather belt. And he was carrying an electronic tablet and a file folder.

"Savannah!" he said, looking surprised and—though she might have been imagining it—miserable at the same time.

"We were just leaving," Savannah said.

"Don't go on our account," Jessica said. "Stay and have dinner. Colin's put together quite the menu—" She stopped short at the menacing look on Colin's face.

"I already know all about it," Savannah said, waving her arm to encompass the whole restaurant. "This was your big lie? That you're a...a restaurant mogul?"

Colin stayed where he was, but Chase turned to Rayne and Jessica and said, "Want to grab a drink at the bar?" They both said yes, and the three of them nearly broke into a run.

When they were gone, Savannah said, "Why didn't you tell me?"

The muscle in Colin's jaw flexed. She's never seen him looking so angry and tired, and she doubted she looked much better. But her heart hurt, and she was getting tired of that feeling.

"So what? Was it all just an elaborate prank or some kind of test to see how long it took me to figure out who you really are?" she asked. "Who else was in on your game?"

He clenched his free hand into a fist, and she was starting to think he wasn't going to answer when he finally said, "I didn't tell you because I wanted to prove to you that what I did for a living didn't matter. We had an instant connection, but as soon as you learned I was just a bartender, you immediately crossed me off your list of datable men."

"That's not—" Savannah started to protest.

"Don't try to say it's not true because you know it is. But it's OK. Because I was actually relieved to meet someone who didn't know I was one of *those* Allisons. It seemed perfect. I'd get you to admit we had a connection and get you to fall for me, I'd know it was for me and not my money, and you'd see that your plan was just silly."

Anger started welling up inside her, mixed with hurt. "You really think I'm that shallow? That I'm only interested in guys for their money and family name?"

"You're the one who was screening dates based on their occupations."

"That's different," she said, her anger taking over now. "I was trying to narrow the field. At least I was upfront about it."

"That doesn't make it any less short-sighted."

The remark stung, but she couldn't back off now. "So you were just pretending to be a bad boy. Did we even need to sneak into the stadium that day?"

"My family owns a concession stand. I showed the security guard my staff ID."

"And Crystal?"

Colin sighed. "I was helping her out of a jam with her supplier. She needed more baking materials than she realized."

Savannah felt like a fool. Diana, Crystal, Chase—they must have had a great time laughing behind her back.

"I knew that whole day was make-believe," she said, sounding more wounded than she would have liked.

"You were pretending, too," he shot back. "Pretending to be

someone who doesn't need to check a spreadsheet before she sleeps with someone."

Savannah's mouth opened in a little O of surprise, and she flushed bright red at his words—and at the sight of a well-dressed older couple who'd come to a stop behind Colin.

"Hello, Colin," the man said. "I hope we're not interrupting anything."

Colin's expression switched from anger to something closer to exhaustion, and he closed his eyes for a moment before slowly turning to face the couple.

"Hello, Dad, Mom," he said.

His father had sharp features and the erect bearing of a military man, and his suit looked like it cost more than Savannah's entire wardrobe. He was staring at Colin with a cold expression, but his mother put her arms around her son and hugged him tight.

"I love what you've done with the place, sweetie," she said, beaming and gesturing around. "The natural lighting, the raw wood decor—it's all fantastic."

Then her gaze came to rest on Savannah. She held out her hand and said, "Bea Allison. And you are...?"

It took Savannah a moment to find her voice. "Savannah. Savannah George."

"It's a pleasure, my dear. And this is my husband Henry."

Colin's dad glanced at her, but his expression didn't change, and he didn't acknowledge Savannah other than to glance at her and then away. For a split second, Savannah thought she might understand why Colin had wanted to hide his family from her, or at least his father.

"I reserved a table for us in the back," Colin told his parents, "where we'll have a little more privacy."

"Yes, private matters should be discussed in private," Henry said.

And Savannah thought the evening couldn't get any more humiliating.

Fortunately, Chase chose that moment to stroll over from the bar, with Jessica and Rayne right behind him.

"Chase!" his mother squealed with delight. "I was afraid you wouldn't make it."

"Hi, Mom," Jessica said, smiling and giving her mother a kiss on the cheek. "Remember me?"

"Oh, of course I do, pumpkin, but I see you all the time, while Chase here—"

"Relax, Mom," Chase said, putting his arm around her. "I'll be in town for a least a month." He winked at Rayne. "Maybe even two."

Rayne blushed and sidled over to stand next to Savannah. In a low voice, she said, "How are you doing?"

"Can we *please* get the hell out of here?"

"Absolutely." Rayne linked her arm through Savannah's, flashed a bright smile at the Allison clan, and said, "It was so nice to see you all, but we've got to take off now." And without waiting for a reply, she guided Savannah to the door.

Chapter 23

A waitress walked up and offered to show the Allisons to their table. As they headed for the rear of the restaurant, Jessica hung back with Colin.

"So I'm guessing things didn't go so well with Savannah," she said, resting a hand on his shoulder.

"Nope."

"Want to get drunk later and talk about it?"

"Nope."

"Well, the good news is that you still get to do your presentation for Dad!" she said with jazz hands.

"Yippee!"

As they reached the table, their father said, "So nice of you to join us."

Colin ignored the comment and signaled to the waitress, who came straight to the table with the cranberry brie crostinis that had been a huge hit when he tested them out at Zipped, along with prosciutto-wrapped mozzarella cubes on toothpicks.

"So you're not giving us a full tasting menu, just some appetizers? Interesting approach," Henry said as he took the glass of red wine out of the waitress' hand before she could set it down.

"Oh, Henry, really," Bea said with an expression that made Jessica choke on her crostini.

Colin didn't react, and a moment later, another waiter arrived with freshly baked rosemary focaccia and three dipping oils. "And when we're done with these, another tray will arrive," Colin said. "Rest assured, Dad, you'll have the full tasting menu experience tonight." Colin forced a smile before taking a long sip of his wine.

Then he took a deep breath and tried to focus his thoughts

and control his emotions so he could make sure this meeting went well. Whenever a new restaurant opened, his father made the general manager—in this case, Colin—explain his plan for profitability and success, which basically meant repeating back Henry's own strategy for profitability and success. With most GMs, it was just for show, just so they knew that Henry Allison was more than a name on their paycheck and he was watching them. But with Colin, it was much more personal, and normally Colin was an expert at charming his father and not letting his gruff mannerisms distract him. But he'd been off his game since losing Savannah, and that scene a few minutes ago definitely didn't help.

His father owned only five percent of Balance&Bite—the minimum ownership required for a restaurant to be part of the Allison Inc. umbrella. Colin had put up most of the money himself from the profits he'd earned at Zipped, and the rest came from Chase and Jessica. He had debated taking this restaurant outside his father's reach, but there were too many advantages to being part of the family conglomerate. And despite how frustrating his father could be, Colin recognized the benefit of having his input and meeting his high standards.

Colin went over his marketing plan and projected profit and loss statement for the first year, knowing his dad had nothing to object to. He made his case thoroughly and clearly, but all the while, he was thinking about how tired Savannah had looked and how her mascara was smeared as if she'd been crying. And though he couldn't recall everything she'd said, the anger and hurt had come through loud and clear.

His father set down his wine glass, wiped his mouth with his napkin, and nodded.

"I can't argue with the quality of the wine or the food," he said, "and the numbers certainly seem to be in order."

That was high praise from his father, and Colin started to smile in relief.

"But I am concerned about your ability to meet these projections when your personal life seems so volatile."

Colin sat back in his chair and took a deep breath, knowing

that it wasn't worth arguing with his father but wanting to do it anyway. "My personal life has never interfered with business."

"The kind of scene we walked in on might fly at Zipped, but it's not going to work here."

Colin felt the heat rise in his face and was about to tell his father to go to hell when Jessica put a hand on his arm to stop him.

"Henry, I think you've made your point," Bea said. "Why don't you wait until there is an actual problem to fuss about before you start to fuss?"

"Fine," Henry said. "I'll fuss about a real problem then." Turning back to Colin, he said, "I was going over some paperwork with Holly Winslow the other day. I understand there's some inventory discrepancies associated with Zipped, specifically regarding several missing bags of sugar and flour. She said she already had a conversation with you about it. Care to tell me what's going on and why we're suddenly having trouble keeping track of our supplies?"

Colin's jaw twitched, but he forced himself not to fidget or look away. "It was temporarily misplaced. Everything's in order now."

"Misplaced?"

"Yeah, Dad," Chase said, pouring his father another glass of wine and topping off his own. "It's a big operation. Things occasionally get put someplace where no one's looking for them. Haven't you ever lost track of anything—say, a car maybe?"

Jessica and Bea laughed, and even Colin cracked a smile. It was a favorite family story. Back when they were kids, his dad was in charge of multiple restaurants and running himself so ragged that one night he took a cab home because he didn't trust himself to drive. And then the next morning, when the car wasn't in the driveway, he called the cops to report it stolen.

"Very funny, Chase," his father said, but he was smiling, too.

A while later, when everyone had sampled the dark-chocolate-and-orange tart and were saying their goodbyes, Colin leaned over and said to Chase, "Thanks for the save back there."

Chase nodded. "I've got your back, bro. Crystal told me what was going on. She's been worried about you getting into trouble with the old man. She found a new supplier—someone who will let her order smaller amounts more frequently, which should fix her cash flow problem. And she wants to pay you back."

"The money's not the issue," Colin said as they walked through the restaurant. "I've just been so distracted lately that I didn't get a chance to replace the stuff before it showed up as missing."

As they pushed through the door and stepped out onto the sidewalk, Colin said, "And hey, since when are you talking to Crystal? Don't tell me you finally worked up the courage to walk into Sweet Happens."

He playfully punched his brother's arm, and Chase grinned at him. "What choice did I have—her muffins are the best in the city. And that hazelnut coffee is the bomb."

"Just don't break her heart—again," Colin said. "She was finally getting to the point where I could have a whole conversation with her without your name coming up."

"Anything for you, bro. And hey, just so you know, I feel like shit about what I said to Savannah that morning. I should have kept my mouth shut."

Colin shook his head. "It's not your fault. The whole thing was a mess anyway."

"I don't suppose meeting good ol' Henry helped your case any."

"It doesn't matter," Colin said. "She's pretty mad and hurt, and I don't see a way back from here. So I guess that's that. And I've got work to do."

"See you back at the apartment later?" Chase asked.

"'Later' is the key word. I need to check on things at Zipped, then I'll be back here until closing."

With an affectionate first bump, the brothers parted ways. Colin was grateful that he had so much to do and keep track of. It helped him push thoughts of Savannah to the back of his mind, where they could only occasionally surface as a nagging sense of regret.

Chapter 24

The day after her run-in with Colin was Savannah's last workday before the big event on Saturday night. She spent it rechecking her to-do list and seating chart as last-minute changes kept coming in, while making a dizzying number of other decisions. She was running on very little sleep, but the adrenaline kept her going. In fact, if it hadn't been for the situation with Colin, she would have been loving every minute of her day.

Saturday morning, as she walked to her hair appointment, she went through her mental checklist for the millionth time to reassure herself that she could spare some time at a fancy salon to get her hair done, finally convincing herself that it would be faster to have a professional do it anyway.

Ninety minutes later, she stepped back onto the street with her hair pulled up into a twist with loose curls framing her face, surprised at how relaxed and confident she felt.

After stopping at home to pick up her dress, she walked to the community center where they were holding the event just as her boss Sarah was walking up.

"Everything all set?" Sarah asked. Savannah could tell she was trying to sound casual but was actually very nervous.

She smiled at Sarah, determined not to take it personally. "Well," she said as she pulled the door open, "the florists are pulling up now, I see volunteers are already setting up the tables, caterers should be on their way, and we still have a whole three hours until the event starts, so I think we're in good shape."

An hour later, as she and Sarah were helping the florist put pale pink peonies in crystal bowls on each of the tables, Savannah's cell phone buzzed. It was the catering company. At the words "accident" and "totaled," she hurried out onto the sidewalk so she wouldn't lose it in front of Sarah.

"Don't you have another truck?" she said, trying to stay calm and find a solution, but her heart was hammering and her head was starting to hurt.

"It's already out on a job for another customer" was the reply.

"I don't give a damn about your other customer! I need my food here. Now!"

"We will return your down payment, and we'd be happy to help you find another caterer."

"Forget it. I'll do it myself."

She resisted the urge to throw the phone on the ground and stomp on it.

Colin could not stop thinking about his run-in with Savannah the other night. He hated to admit it, but even though they were fighting, he'd still enjoyed being near her. At times, he had trouble recalling exactly what the problem was, and he was starting to wonder if maybe they could just start over.

As he wiped down the already clean bar, lost in thought, he didn't notice that Diana had come in until she said, "I saw your girl on my way over here."

"My girl?" Then it dawned on him. "She's not my girl," he said throwing the rag at a black bin and starting to stack glasses. "Not anymore."

Diana studied him as she picked up an order pad and pen and stuck them in her apron pocket.

"She's at the community center over on 4th," she said. "They're setting up for a party or something. She looked pretty stressed. She was yelling into her phone and waving her arms around like a crazy person."

Colin stopped stacking glasses. "Oh yeah, I think today is her big event. I hope nothing major has gone wrong." He knew he shouldn't care, but he wanted to go check on her.

Diana glanced around at the handful of people in the bar. "I've got this."

Colin looked at her. "What do you mean?"

"Oh, drop the act. I know you're dying to run over there and check on her. So GO. I've got this."

Without another thought, Colin turned and headed for the door, yelling, "Thanks D!" over his shoulder.

As he jogged the four blocks to the community center, he told himself that even if they weren't going to date, they could at least be friends. He'd take that over nothing.

He saw her from a block away, pacing back and forth on the sidewalk while furiously tapping on her phone's screen.

"Are you OK?" he asked when he reached her.

Startled, she stopped pacing and stared at him for a second before laughing a short, humorless laugh.

"I don't need any more drama today."

"No drama, I promise. I just want to help if I can."

"Well, my caterer is stuck in Annapolis with a busted-up truck, so unless you can produce an entire catering staff and food for fifty people from your pocket, we have nothing to talk about."

"Who were you using?" Colin asked, suddenly worried it had been one of the Allisons' outfits.

"Some company that has ties to a board member," she said. "But it doesn't matter because they're in friggin' Annapolis and all they can do is offer excuses, which is worth a whole lot of nothing."

Colin had never seen Savannah this riled up, and despite himself, he found it adorable.

"What time does the party start?"

"Less than two hours. And the donors will have no food or alcohol, which is going to make the whole program a lot less interesting." Savannah had started to pace again, and her voice had gone up an octave. "Is there a Costco near here? Or wait, maybe Ben's Chili Bowl would deliver and we can act like we did it on purpose?"

As she talked, she was feverishly googling options on her phone.

"Were they providing the bar, too?" Colin asked.

She looked up at him as though she was seeing him for the

first time and slowly nodded.

"Tell me exactly what you need," he said.

She suddenly seemed to snap into gear. "We need full bar and fancy heavy appetizers for fifty people starting at 6:00 and lasting for two hours, with coffee and dessert for thirty minutes after that."

Colin nodded as he pulled out his phone. "Linens and tables?"

"We've got all of that from another vendor. We're just missing food, booze, and people to serve it."

"OK. I'll check back with you in half an hour. Just go in and finish getting everything set up," Colin said as he put the phone to his ear.

"Wait, how are you…I mean, you can just—" Savannah stammered.

"I got this, Red. Go back to work." Then he started talking fast into his phone as he jogged away, and after another stunned second, Savannah went back inside.

She told Sarah that the original caterer had bailed but that she'd found an excellent substitute and everything was under control, though the food might be just a tad late. Despite Colin's assurances, she didn't see how he could pull everything together by 6:00, so she hoped he'd at least send over the wine on time.

But thirty minutes later, Colin walked through the door of the community center wearing black dress pants and a T-shirt with a case of wine under his arm and a white dress shirt in a dry-cleaning bag hooked over his fingers. Savannah rushed over to meet him.

"Where's the bar going to be?" he asked.

She pointed to a linen-draped table off to the side and turned to see Chase coming through the door carrying another case of wine. He smiled at Savannah and followed Colin over to the tabled she'd indicated.

For the next hour, more men and women streamed in carrying wine or trays of appetizers that smelled delicious. Colin, Chase, and the other servers soon put on their white dress shirts and black bowties, and Savannah marveled at the transformation and, for the first time in days, started to relax.

Chase walked over to her with a tray of appetizers. "Can I interest the lady in smoked salmon on flatbread?"

Savannah laughed as she picked up one of the snacks. "I'm impressed," she said.

"You don't grow up in the Allison family without knowing how to serve a few hors d'oeuvres," he said with a wink before walking away.

"That's better," Colin said as he came up next to her. "A smiling customer is a happy customer."

"I can't thank you enough. This is...amazing."

"Thank me later. Shouldn't you go get dressed?"

Laughing, she looked down at her dirty leggings and button-down shirt. "What, you don't think this will pass for black tie?" Savannah couldn't ignore the fact that it felt really good to be laughing with Colin again.

"I think you look great, but I can't promise your boss would agree," Colin said with a wink.

"Yeah, plus I spent like a week's salary on this dress, so I'd better get some use out of it," she said with a smile. "Just one thing though. I, um, I didn't see the dessert and coffee come in?" She hated to push since just having any food at all felt like a miracle.

"It will be here any minute."

"I'm here!" Jessica rushed through the door carrying a stack of thin bakery boxes. "Chase! Grab the coffee urns out of the van."

"Yes, ma'am!" Chase said and hurried out the door.

Colin helped Jessica with the boxes, Chase came back with the coffee urns, and Savannah gaped at them as they moved around the room like a finely tuned machine.

"It's kind of a random assortment of desserts from my place and Sweet Happens," Jessica said over her shoulder as she set up the coffee and hot water for tea. "But they should do the trick. Good luck tonight! Bye!" And Jessica was out the door before Savannah could thank her.

Savannah's phone beeped to remind her that the reception was going to start in thirty minutes. Running back to the room where she'd left her dress, she did the fastest wardrobe change of her life, and fifteen minutes later, she walked back into the party room dressed in a knee-length navy blue cocktail dress that crossed her chest in a deep V, hugged her waist, and flared slightly to the knee.

Colin noticed her the minute she walked back into the room, and the sight of her took his breath away. Even from this distance, he could see that the navy dress made her eyes turn a deep, entrancing emerald color. He watched from behind the makeshift bar as she moved rapidly around the room making sure everything was in place, the click of her high heels echoing the beating of his heart.

As Savannah hurried around the room checking and rechecking every detail, she tried not to look for Colin. She told herself she didn't care what he thought of her dress and wished she still had a rubber band on her wrist to snap. Clearly he had no interest in her after their little scene the other night. She was still trying to hold onto her indignation and anger that he'd lied to her, but the truth was that she could see why he had. She may have gotten a little obsessed with the dating part of The Plan. But Colin had thrown her off balance since the moment she'd met him. Her attraction to him was so strong it had to lead somewhere bad. The Plan was her protection.

"You look amazing." Colin's soft and familiar voice broke into Savannah's thoughts, and she spun around to find him standing close enough that she could smell the fancy cologne he was wearing in place of his normal earthy, soapy smell.

Smiling and resisting the urge to fidget with her dress, she gestured to the room. "I can't believe you did all this on such short notice."

Colin waved her words away. "You'd better go. If you need anything, I'll be behind the bar."

Then he took a step backward, hands in his pockets, looking

sexier than should be legal, and said, "Knock 'em dead, Red."

Savannah took one last survey of the room. Food stations had been set up around the room, waiters were stationed strategically with trays of appetizers and glasses of wine, and the bar was beautifully appointed. She didn't think anyone would be able to tell this had been a last-minute job.

Sarah joined Savannah. "Everything looks incredible," she said. "I don't know how you managed to get another caterer in here so quick, but I'm impressed. Outstanding job."

Savannah flushed with pride and glanced toward the bar. Colin gave her a thumbs-up and a smile, and her heart started to melt. But she had no time to think about it because the guests were starting to arrive.

The evening passed in a blur of smiles, applause, and delicious food. And seeing Colin behind the bar had the surprising effect of keeping her calm and centered. As the last of the guests were leaving, Sarah said, "That was a well-run event, Savannah. First rate. I think you've got a very bright future at the Capitol Foundation."

"Thank you, Sarah. I'm so happy you're happy with how it went," Savannah said. She felt exhilarated, but she also felt exhaustion starting to creep up on her.

"I hope you don't mind, but I need to take off. I figured you could handle the cleanup, especially since it looks like that sexy bartender has taken care of most of it already," Sarah said with a smile. "He didn't take his eyes off you the entire night—even as he poured drinks and charmed every person he talked to. He's quite a multi-tasker."

Savannah glanced over at Colin, who was packing up the leftover wine bottles. "Yeah, he's a pretty good guy."

"Why don't you take Monday off? You've earned it," Sarah said. "I'll see you in the office on Tuesday."

After she left, Savannah walked over to Colin.

"What can I do to help?" she asked.

"It's all under control," Colin said as he handed the last of the garbage bags to one of the waitresses. The woman walked out the door, and Savannah was suddenly alone with Colin. Her heart beat faster, and a blush started to creep up her neck.

"Well, Red, I'd say you pulled it off," he said.

He was smiling a little awkwardly, and his hands were shoved in his pockets. Savannah realized that he was nervous, too. She knew that when he was happy his eyes became a brighter blue, and when he was mad, they turned almost indigo and he got a little crease across his forehead. She remembered the sound he made in the back of his throat when he was really turned on. And, she realized with a stab, she knew what he looked like when he was heartbroken.

And she knew that when his eyes crinkled at the edges and the muscle in his jaw twitched, like it did now, it was because he was anxious.

"OK, well, I should probably get going." Colin started to walk away, and Savannah realized she'd been staring at him without speaking for the last minute or so.

"No! Wait," she said, putting her hand on his arm. "I wanted to… I mean, I can't believe …" Savannah stopped talking, took a breath and tried again. "I mean, thank you. Thank you for doing all of this. I don't know how…I couldn't have…" As the words started to tumble out in a disordered mess again, her face grew redder and her eyes filled with tears.

"Hey, hey, hey," Colin said softly, closing his hand over hers. "Everything turned out great. There's no reason to get upset."

Savannah sniffled and looked at him through a haze of tears, suddenly overcome with fatigue. "After those awful things I accused you of, you still…you saved me."

He put his strong arms around her, and she pressed her face to his chest, and all the stress and tension and heartache that she had been holding in for weeks let loose and the tears poured out.

"I'm sorry," she sobbed as he kissed the top of her head. "I'm so, so sorry."

Colin held her tight until she stopped shaking. Then he pulled back to look into her face. "I'm sorry, too," he said. "I should have told you the truth about everything. I never should have lied to you."

"It doesn't matter," she said. "Let's just forget all of it. Can we? Can we just start fresh?"

"Under one condition," he said.

"Anything."

"You have to promise to stop all the crying because I swear, woman, your tears are going to be the death of me."

Savannah laughed with relief and then her gaze fell on Colin's once-white shirt, now covered with streaks and splotches of makeup.

"I ruined your shirt," she said, running her fingers over a mascara stain.

"It was worth it." He swiped his thumb under her eyes to wipe away leftover tears and leaned in to kiss her softly.

Savannah slid her hand around to the back of his neck and deepened the kiss, surprised again at how intense her attraction was. Then, pulling back slightly, she ran her hand along his jaw.

"There are no more secrets, right?" she asked.

"None. Ever," Colin said immediately. With a smile Savannah pulled him to her for another kiss.

"I do have one question though," he said as he trailed kisses down her neck to her collarbone.

"Uh huh," she murmured, wondering if anyone was left in the building or if she could just tear his clothes off where they stood.

"What about The Plan?"

"The plan right now is to keep doing this and maybe a little of this," she said, trailing her hand down his stomach to the waistband of his pants.

Chuckling softly, Colin said, "I definitely support that plan. But what about *The* Plan. The one that has controlled everything since we met."

"Ah, right. That Plan," Savannah said dropping her eyes and studying her silver shoes.

He put a finger under her chin and lifted her face so he could look into her eyes. "I'm not Jake, you know."

"Jake? How do you know—"

"Rayne told me," Colin said. "She was worried about you,

about us. Don't be mad at her. It helped me understand better what was going on with you."

"Well, I guess I owe her one," Savannah said with a small smile, as she played with the buttons on the front of his shirt.

"So is The Plan still in charge?"

"I think it's time the plan got a bit of a rewrite."

"I'm listening," he said with a smile.

"I was going to start by changing 'suit-wearing bureaucrat' to 'sexy, tattooed restaurant mogul.'"

"Good call," he said while leaning in to nuzzle her neck. "What else?"

Savannah let out a moan, but she tried to keep her thoughts in order for just a moment longer. "I'm just deleting the rest because where I live or work doesn't matter."

"Oh yeah? Then what does matter?"

Savannah put her hands on either side of Colin's jaw and held his face so she could look into his eyes. "That I have a guy who makes me laugh and feel safe and like I'm the most important person in his life. The type of man I want by my side every day because nothing makes sense without him."

Colin rested his forehead against hers while running his hands up and down her back. "Nothing makes sense without you either. God, Savannah, I'm so in love with you."

Savannah traced a finger along his lips. "Good. Because I'm in love with you, too."

Colin leaned forward and pulled her into a deep, smoldering kiss, and just before she lost control, she shredded The Plan into tiny pieces in her mind and let the wind blow them away.

Check out the Capitol Love Series Book 2:

The Pursuit...

Rayne Michael has built her life around stability. After a vagabond upbringing, she has carefully built a predictable and satisfying life between her Washington, D.C., neighborhood of Capitol Hill and her job at a small conservation group. But when her organization's survival is threatened, her only option is to hatch a plan to save it with a charming, sexy, and totally unreliable man she can't seem to stay away from.

Chase Allison is a freelance nature photographer whose work takes him around the world on a moment's notice, which suits him just fine—especially when he wants to shake loose from a relationship. Which he generally does after a few weeks of fun. Yet he is strangely captivated by Rayne and the passion that lurks behind her smoky gray eyes, but can his attraction compete with the allure of the open road?

And can Rayne find a way to balance her need for stability with her need to be with free-spirited Chase?

About the Author

Samantha Powers lived in the Washington, D.C., area for several years and worked in various corporate and nonprofit jobs while writing in her spare time. She now lives in Vermont, where she can indulge her passion for walks in the woods, writing full time, and maple-flavored everything. She also loves animals, reality TV, and cupcakes.

Her short story "Portrait of a Lover" appears in the *Trick or Treat!* anthology published in October 2015.

Follow her on Twitter: @CapitolLover or
Facebook: CapitolLoveSeries